The hairs on the [...] Mack Bolan's ne[...] stood up

The streets leading to the house looked normal, placid, but the Executioner knew something wasn't right. He turned to run, but three punks in black leather jumped from the bushes to block his way with their shotguns. Bolan heard others move in from behind.

He turned in a slow circle. Shotguns were pointed at him from windows and doorways, from behind trees and shrubs.

Bolan stood silent and raised his arms. The front door to the house opened, and Dr. Mett walked slowly toward him. The doctor's face showed no emotion.

Dr. Mett stared at Bolan as he pulled a pistol from his jacket. He raised it slowly, aiming high, and pulled the trigger.

Mack Bolan heard the sound, felt the flare of pain in his head. Then he whirled steadily downward into a pool of the calmest, blackest night.

MACK BOLAN

The Executioner

DON PENDLETON's EXECUTIONER
MACK BOLAN
Code of Dishonor

A GOLD EAGLE BOOK FROM
W☉RLDWIDE

TORONTO • NEW YORK • LONDON • PARIS
AMSTERDAM • STOCKHOLM • HAMBURG
ATHENS • MILAN • TOKYO • SYDNEY

First edition March 1987

ISBN 0-373-61099-8

Special thanks and acknowledgment to
Mike McQuay for his contribution to this work.

Printed in Canada

Hold it the greatest wrong to prefer life to honor and for the sake of life to lose the reason for living.

—Juvenal

He has honor if he holds himself to an ideal of conduct though it is inconvenient, unprofitable, or dangerous to do so.

—Walter Lippmann

Honor is actually a physical thing—the heart to know what's right, the guts to do what's right and the muscle to back it up.

—Mack Bolan

PROLOGUE

Staff Sergeant Wilson Loomis wheeled the dark blue jeep from behind the Air Police shack at the front gate and gunned it across the hard-packed dirt to Freedom Boulevard, which bisected the Fremont Air Base in South Dakota.

"Crap," said Peterson from beside him as they bounced onto the floodlit road, a cloud of white dust following them. "Why don't they pave us a road back over there?"

Loomis smiled over at the other AP. "Then you wouldn't have nothin' to complain about, Sarge."

"Crap," Peterson said again, and his hand went reflexively to the billy club at his side.

They sped past the double rows of barracks that lined both sides of the road, then turned onto Mitchell, just past the BX, and hurried toward the commotion at the NCO Club. The land stretched out flat and wide into the darkness in all directions. Silos filled with near-obsolete Minuteman missiles pitted the barren landscape. It was a cold Dakota night, and once again Loomis wished he had drawn duty in Hawaii.

"Travis is gonna have his bowels in an uproar over this one," Peterson said. "He's been trying to shut down the club for a year 'cause of gamblin', and a big fight ain't gonna make it any easier to keep it open."

"Look!" Loomis said, pointing. The club sat a block down the road. A crowd had gathered around the large wooden structure, and flames were shooting out one of the windows, smoke drifting into the night sky.

Loomis felt his muscles tighten, and his own hand went to the club at his side, his bright white gloves standing out under the glare of the floodlights. "Call for backup," he began, "and get one of the crash cars over here."

He reached down and hit the siren, turning on the cherry that sat on the roof. He could hear Peterson on the radio as he used his horn to part the large crowd that blocked the street.

They skidded to a stop by the wide front steps of the building, their headlights coming to rest on a body sprawled across the stairs.

"Crap," Peterson muttered as they climbed out of the jeep. He ran to the body while Loomis addressed the crowd.

"I want anybody who was in there to come up here by the jeep!" he called loudly as he unholstered his is-sue .45. "The rest of you get out of here!"

Not surprisingly, everyone moved into the safety of the darkness, which was all Loomis wanted, anyway. A halfhearted bucket brigade had formed and was throwing buckets of water through the window where the flames shot out. He turned to see Peterson sitting on the stairs, staring at his hand. He walked over to the man.

"It's Isley," Peterson said, pointing to the man on the stairs. He held up a hand. His white glove was soaked with blood. "He's dead."

Loomis bent toward Master Sergeant Ted Isley, NCO in charge of the base club, and rolled him over. The man's stomach had been shredded with an SMG; blood and intestines leaked from a series of open wounds. There was no doubt of his condition.

"Good God," Loomis said. Isley's eyes were wide open, a look of perplexity on his face that Loomis couldn't stand to see. He rolled the man back over to hide that face.

Peterson stood and looked into the open doorway. "We got to go in there?" he asked.

Loomis nodded and moved up the stairs. In the distance he could hear approaching sirens—backup. His stomach was in knots as he moved to the right of the doorway, motioning Peterson to the other side. They jumped through the doorway, hitting the floor and rolling into a crouch with their weapons extended before them.

Loomis had spent nearly every night in the club during the past year and a half—there had been little else to do in such godforsaken country—yet he hardly recognized it. The smoke and flames and flickering lights had turned it into a landscape from a nightmare. The sound of the jukebox provided eerie background music.

He stood slowly, cautiously, and Peterson followed his lead.

"I don't like this, Will," the man said.

"Go pull the plug on that damned machine," Loomis said, blinking against the smoke and moving forward.

The place was a wreck, with overturned tables and chairs and broken glass scattered everywhere. There had been more than just a fight here.

He tripped, falling hard against a table before regaining his footing. Loomis had stumbled over another body, a body dressed in civilian clothes.

He retched, vomiting on the dirty wooden floor, and was white as milk when he stood up.

"Sweet Jesus," came Peterson's voice from across the smoke-filled room. "Oh, no."

"Pete? Where are you?"

He made his way to the dining room. His eyes were beginning to burn.

"Loomis?" came a voice from the direction of the doorway. More APs had arrived.

"In here," Loomis called. "Get ambulances. Come in careful, but watch for me and Peterson."

"Gotcha."

Loomis made the dining room, the music still rising and falling from the jukebox. The sight was sickening. He closed his eyes, pressing his handkerchief tightly against his mouth to keep from screaming. That music. That damned music was still droning.

"No!" he yelled finally, snapping under the strain. He turned and began firing at the jukebox, emptying the clip into the phonograph. And finally it died, fading slowly away.

Loomis looked down the dark hallway, and instinctively he knew that the battle had started there. "The back room," he said and reached out to slap Peterson on the arm. "Let's check it."

The man nodded, and they moved into the hallway, stepping across the civilian body that lay there. The back room was where the gambling took place, where the booze was drunk after hours, where the pot was smoked. This was where the noncoms came when they wanted to be bad little boys.

"Watch it," he said and brought up a booted foot.

Peterson hugged the wall as Loomis kicked viciously at the door, tearing it right off its hinges.

Five bodies lay just inside the door of the gaming room. In the flickering light Loomis could see a crap table, its surface covered by what looked like a pile of sand. He reached the table and discovered that a small mountain of white powder was piled on it. It wasn't sand. It sure as hell wasn't sugar. He touched the side of the pile, coming away with a dusting that he brought to his tongue.

It was bitter, harsh, and within seconds he began losing the feeling in his tongue. Cocaine.

Loomis backed away in awe. He had no idea how much cocaine sold for, but he knew he was looking at millions of dollars' worth. It didn't take a genius to figure out what had gone down in the club. Master Sergeant Isley had tried to move the powder to the civilian pushers, and a greedy fight had broken out.

Loomis stared at the small mountain of coke on the table. He couldn't help but wonder at the power it wielded.

The old Hank Williams record scratched through a high-tech sound system as Mack Bolan nursed a coffee at the bar of the Japanese clip joint. The voice of the country singer did little to soothe Bolan's uneasiness.

Hillbilly Heaven was located in an area known as Bar Row, less than a mile from the main gates of Yokota Air Base. It was a phone booth-sized serviceman's bar, squeezed into a two-block area with dozens of other bars just like it. Twenty-seven miles from Tokyo propcr, Hillbilly Heaven could just as easily have been in Manila or Panama City or Bangkok or... Saigon. The cities and bars were all the same, with the same country music, the same lonely farm boys, the same bar girls, the same overpriced "tea" they served that encouraged the blond kids from Nebraska to talk about their confusion.

Bolan felt confused. There was something about this whole deal that didn't make sense. It was out of his control, and control was everything in his line of work.

He smelled the woman's perfume before she reached him, and he glanced up to watch her reflection in the mirror behind the counter. She was a bar girl. Her black hair fell below her bare shoulders, and the slit of her tight red dress exposed a shapely thigh.

"Would you like to buy me a drink, big man?" she asked.

"Go find somebody else," he said as he looked at his watch. It was 8:00 p.m. Something should be happening.

She squeezed his shoulder with her red-nailed fingers. "You don't like girls?"

"I like girls fine," he said and turned to stare at her. She returned his cold gaze fearlessly and moved closer, her hands going to his chest. Bolan knew he was being patted down by an expert, and he didn't think it was his wallet she was interested in.

"What do you want?" he asked, grabbing her wrist before her fingertips touched the butt of the Beretta 93-R nestled in its combat harness under his light jacket.

A smile just touched her lips then fled. "You Mr. Reeves?"

"Yeah," he said softly.

"I have a message for you from—"

He put a hand on her mouth. "Let's take a walk," he said.

"But my boss . . ."

He stopped her with a look, then reached into his pocket and threw a hundred-dollar bill on the polished bar. "Outside," he said.

He took her by the arm and led her outside as several airmen belted out "Your Cheatin' Heart" along with the record. Bolan wondered if he had ever been that young.

They moved into the Japanese night, the narrow, winding street lit by the gaudy neon signs advertising each drinking establishment. The place looked like a carnival.

The street was wet; it was the rainy season, early summer, and the dampness had seeped into everything. He directed the woman into a quiet corner and then turned her to face him. She was young, probably still a teenager.

"What have you got?"

"You're supposed to meet a man in a red cap at the pachinko parlor on the corner of Nishi-Ginza."

He took her arms, squeezing hard. "Tell me the truth," he demanded, and fright finally filled her eyes.

"An old man come this afternoon," she said quickly. "He tell me to look for Mr. Reeves at eight o'clock and to give him the message, and he gave me a thousand yen. That's all."

She was trembling. Bolan didn't believe for a moment that she was frightened of him, but he did believe her story. He let her go, and her manner softened as she raised her hands to massage her arms.

"You hurt me," she said.

Bolan reached into his pocket for a hundred-dollar bill like the one he'd given her boss. It was the government's money. He was simply using it as hands-on foreign aid.

Her eyes lit up, and she snatched the bill. "This a lot of cash," she said, looking around. "Maybe you want something else for it?"

He looked at her, remembering a girl no older than this one, a young woman who had been unselfish and kind. "Go home and give that money to your family," he said. Although his sister had been gone for many years, the pain of her forced prostitution and subsequent death still burned within him. "Don't flash it around if you want to keep it."

"You don't worry about me," she said with youthful arrogance as she slipped the bill down her bodice. "Mari take care of herself, Mr. Reeves."

She turned then and hurried away before he could change his mind, and Bolan was alone again. Reeves was the name on his passport, one of many identities that he'd had in the past twenty years. In Nam they had called him Sergeant Mercy. The last time he'd been to Japan, they'd called him Colonel Phoenix. And there was another name for which he was well known—the Executioner.

Bolan moved down to the end of the block and turned onto Meiji-Dori, heading away from the base. He knew where the pachinko parlor was. He had done a recon of the whole area during the daylight hours, just in case he needed to get away quickly. Japan is a country of many mountains and streets that wind in and out like jungle paths, an easy place for most Westerners to lose their way. Under the circumstances, Bolan wanted every advantage he could get.

He walked slowly, watching. It was the end of the month, so most of the GIs were out of money and staying away from Bar Row. Only gangs of Japanese youths, who prowled their territories like panthers, roamed the streets. Straight ahead, barely defined in the darkness, Mount Fuji towered over the Tokyo landscape.

He kept moving, trying to walk out his apprehensions about the mission. It had been called Operation Snowflake, but who—or what—it was, no one knew. There was something about a cocaine smuggling ring operating within the Air Force, but death had stilled the connecting voices and Internal Security had failed to turn up anything about the operation. But then there had been the call from the American Embassy in Tokyo. The embassy had received a message from a hysterical Japanese national who claimed to have information about Operation Snowflake. But the man wouldn't divulge anything until he was protected. Hal Brognola had called Bolan and asked him if he could handle a clandestine mission that couldn't be trusted to government channels.

Bolan rarely trusted anything to government channels. He operated alone, waging a personal war against those who would take away the freedom and lives of innocent people. In his war of attrition, the petty bickering and compromises of governments held no sway. Mack Bolan was justice, swift justice with cold blue eyes. He was death itself to those who deserved it—the drug pushers, the loan sharks, the terrorists. Hunted by every government and law-enforcement agency in the world, he continued his work with the help of a few good people who cared, including Hal Brognola.

Bolan's attention was diverted to a roaring Honda .950 ridden by a Japanese youth dressed in black leather and an opaque black helmet. A red circle was fixed on the left breast pocket of the punk's jacket.

The rider stopped ten feet away from Bolan, blocking his path. Bolan kept walking, ignoring him. The rider turned to watch, although Bolan could not see his eyes through the black visor of the helmet. When Bolan got right up to him, the youth gunned the engine and sped off into the night.

The pachinko parlor was just ahead, a well-lit establishment with Japanese neon characters dancing up and down the sides of the building, the only thing open in this quieter section of town.

As Bolan approached the building, he couldn't shake the uneasy feeling that had been with him for some time. Nothing about this mission made any sense.

He drew a long breath and then walked into the building and into layers of cigarette smoke and a never-ending clacking sound. Row upon row of pachinko machines filled the place, many of them operated by old men who kept feeding small ball bearings into their fronts. Then they'd turn a dial, shooting a marble-sized steel ball up to the top of the machine. Gravity pulled the ball onto a series of ornately arranged pegs where it would bounce crazily down the length of the machine and either fall to the bottom or into one of the payoff holes where the operator would be rewarded with another handful of ball bearings. The players fed the balls one after another so that each second another ball began the course.

Bolan had been in one of these places before. People addicted to this particular form of recreation would arrive early in the morning and stay, transfixed, until closing time, sometimes amassing several buckets of ball bearings that they could trade for merchandise inside the parlor. The authorities didn't consider pachinko to be gambling, which Bolan knew was illegal in Japan.

He moved deeper into the noise and the garish yellow lighting. The building had ten rows of back-to-back machines, each row containing perhaps twenty units. The men operating them sat tightly together, their shoulders bumping with each pull of the lever. Bolan moved slowly, cautiously, along the rows, searching for a man in a red hat.

Why here? Bolan wondered. What did this place have to do with cocaine in South Dakota? Bolan moved slowly, nearly mesmerized by the hypnotic action of the tumbling balls, when all at once he was staring directly at a Philadelphia Phillies baseball cap atop the head of a small old man.

The man fed his balls quickly from a bucket at his feet that was nearly filled. Bolan was sure the small man had been there for many hours. He talked to himself in a singsong cadence, moving slowly back and forth as he plugged the balls into the machine's small opening.

"I'm Reeves," Bolan said, but the man couldn't hear him over the noise. "I'm Reeves!" Bolan said loudly, and the man turned to him, shaking his head, his eyes laughing.

"You come!" he exclaimed, turning from the machine and bowing to Bolan.

Bolan stared down at the man. "Can we go somewhere to talk?"

"Are you with the CIA?" the man asked loudly.

Bolan put a finger to his lips. "Not exactly," he said, and the man frowned, obviously disappointed that he didn't merit the royal treatment. "Let's go somewhere," Bolan requested again.

The man shook his head. "No, no," he said. "I get no time to play anymore. We talk here. No one listen."

Bolan looked around. No one was watching them; everyone was engrossed in their own game. "You're the man who called the embassy?"

The old man flicked dark eyes toward him that were lost in wrinkles. He wore baggy khaki pants and a well-worn plaid shirt. "Yes, that was me, yes."

"Why?"

The man shook his head, his stare fixed on the tumbling balls. One fell in the payoff slot and a score of balls dropped into the bucket with a loud rattle. "Much danger," he said. "They look for us...to kill us."

"Look for who?"

"Me!" the man said emphatically. "Me and Dr. Norwood."

"Who is Dr. Norwood?"

The old man looked at him, exasperated, as one would look at a bothersome child. "Dr. Norwood, Dr. Norwood...Operation Snowflake. I am his valet and trusted assistant, Toshu Maruki." The man bowed again quickly, then went back to his game. "So, you will save us and give us asylum?"

"Tell me about the cocaine," Bolan said, his mouth very close to the man's ear.

Maruki looked at him quizzically. "Co...caine?" he said slowly, thinking hard. "What is co...caine?"

Bolan stared at him. Could there be some mistake, a mix-up of words? He knew for certain that he wasn't going to get anything sensible from Maruki. "Where is Dr. Norwood?" he asked.

The man looked at him again and he stopped feeding balls into the machine. "Please, Mr. Reeves. They are very powerful. Will you save us? Will you please to save us?"

"I'll do my best," Bolan said, the man's plea sounding strangely hopeless. He looked around again.

The whole front of the building was plate glass, affording him a good view of the street. An Air Force jeep had pulled up farther down the block. Three APs sat in the open vehicle, despite the steady drizzle. "But you're going to have to tell me where I can find Dr. Norwood."

The old man searched Bolan's eyes. Apparently satisfied with what he saw there, he said quickly, "Fujikyu Shrine. We go from here?"

"The sooner, the better," Bolan said, and the old man bent to pick up his bucket of balls. Bolan stopped him. "Leave them."

As they started back down the aisle, a leather boy like the one Bolan had seen on the street came in the front door. Bolan immediately turned toward the door at the side of the building but was blocked by another black-clad biker.

Bolan reached for his Beretta just as the punk at the door pulled the .12-gauge Remington pump from behind him and fired into the building. All at once six armed bikers pushed their way into the building and opened fire.

Pandemonium broke loose with the first shot; old men screamed and ran back and forth in the enclosed room. As Bolan went into a crouch, he tried to drag Maruki down with him.

The punks ran through the building firing indiscriminately. Pops like a string of firecrackers flashed throughout the room, filling it with the smell of gunpowder. A man staggered past them, blood oozing between the fingers that held his face. Pachinko machines exploded, showering glass and ball bearings over everything.

Maruki, confused and frightened, broke from Bolan's grasp and tried to run. Bolan jumped up to grab him, but he slipped on the steel balls that littered the floor and went down hard.

Punks were at both ends of the aisle. Bolan couldn't get a clear shot in the confusion. There were too many innocents in his line of fire. That didn't bother the enemy gunmen who hammered away in obvious enjoyment. Maruki screamed as his chest exploded. The small Japanese man was dead before his body fell on Bolan.

Bolan got to his feet. A shotgun came up behind him. He wheeled and fired as the punk ducked away. And then everything stopped—deathly quiet. Within thirty seconds it was over.

Then Bolan saw why. One of the bikers had tossed a large satchel into the room as his friends scattered. It had to be explosives!

"Run!" Bolan screamed and knew instinctively that he couldn't reach the bag before it went up. Several aisles separated him from the now shattered plate-glass window. He threw himself at a machine, knocking it and the one behind it over as he fell into the next aisle. Pain shot through his arm, but he jumped up and crossed to the next aisle the same way. Another aisle and he had reached the window. Cut now in several places, he jumped through the window, coming down hard on glass in the street outside.

Bolan was up, staggering in the rain, his Beretta covered with his own blood. Old men were staggering through the doors and windows, trying to get away as motorcycles roared off down the narrow street.

Bolan ran, trying to put as much distance between himself and the building as he could. He got no more than ten steps when the concussion from a monstrous explosion knocked him to the pavement.

The entire building burst open with a loud whomp and a rush of wind as a flash of bright orange and black lit up the dull sky. A million ball bearings shot like bullets from ground zero. People on the streets fell, torn to shreds as the deadly pellets lit up the night, sparkling brightly, ricocheting off streets, lampposts, cars and surrounding buildings.

Bolan lay on the ground with his head covered. Within seconds the pachinko balls began falling from the sky like metal rain, clicking loudly on the streets and cars, bouncing as they hit the pavement. And when all the noise stopped, Mack Bolan rolled over and checked himself for damage.

He was cut up pretty good, blood oozing thickly from a large gash in his left hand. He took out a handkerchief and wrapped it around the wound. All around him people were moaning and checking themselves for injuries. Some were standing, trying to help others to their feet.

The entire building housing the pachinko parlor had collapsed; small fires burned in the rubble. Several cars were overturned nearby, and one of them had burst into flames. The dead lay everywhere. The innocent victims. It was always the same.

Bolan was trying to stand when he heard the roar of an engine. He turned to see the jeepful of APs driving toward him. Where were they when the fighting had been going on? he wondered. Bolan quickly stuck the Beretta back in his holster and stood as the jeep stopped right beside him.

"You guys are a little bit slow. I—"

"Shut up!" one of them yelled, and they were out of the jeep, pressing around him. Someone grabbed his arms, and as he twisted to throw the man off, the side of his head exploded in a brilliant white flash from the force of a billy club.

Bolan dropped to his knees, teeth clenched with the blinding pain. He raised his head and looked directly into the muzzle of a .45 automatic.

"Kill him," the master sergeant said.

2

The tech sergeant grinned and primed the .45 with a loud snap. The Executioner barely had a second to appreciate the irony of being gunned down in an alien land by representatives of the country he had given so much of his life to defend.

And then a siren broke through his thoughts.

"Son of a bitch!" the master sergeant said, and Bolan turned his head, looking through the legs of the men surrounding him to see a Japanese police car screech onto Nishi-Ginza, its pale blue cherry throwing light into the drizzly sky.

"Grab him," the master sergeant said, and the men jumped to take Bolan's arms. "We'll take him with us."

Still weak and disoriented from the blow to his head, Bolan was no match for the APs, who twisted his arms hard behind him.

The police car pulled up beside them as the master sergeant walked up to Bolan. He was a big man, six foot four or five, with a nasty scowl etched permanently on his face. The name O'Brian was written on his name tag. Mack Bolan memorized everything about him.

"Keep your mouth shut tight," O'Brian said, then reached into Bolan's jacket to retrieve the Beretta. He found Bolan's .44 AutoMag—Big Thunder—in the side holster below it. "Lookee here," he told the other two. "This boy's got him some hardware."

The Japanese police were out of their car, and a clean-cut detective wearing a suit was barking orders in Japanese to his uniformed squad. One man jumped back in the vehicle and frantically put through a call on his radio, and two others ran over toward the building to try to help the survivors.

"Let's go!" O'Brian yelled, and Bolan's captors dragged him toward their jeep.

Bolan made a quick decision. "No!" he yelled loudly. "What are you doing?"

"Damn you," O'Brian rasped as he threw a sharp elbow into Bolan's stomach, causing him to double over. "Get him in the jeep, quick!"

"Wait," the plainclothes cop said in perfect English. "What's going on?"

He hurried over to the jeep, a look of concern crossing his face as he took in Bolan's condition.

O'Brian stepped between the cop and Bolan. "Master Sergeant Tom O'Brian, Yokota Air Police," he said in an officious tone.

"Lieutenant Ichiro, Special Services, Tokyo Police," the smaller man said. "What's going on here?"

O'Brian was much taller than Ichiro and he moved closer to the man, trying to intimidate him. But Ichiro stood his ground, hands on hips.

"This man is an airman from the base," O'Brian said. "We've suspected him of terrorist activities and followed him here tonight. He may have caused this explosion. We're taking him back to the base for questioning."

"Those weapons..." Ichiro said, pointing to Bolan's guns.

"Found them on him," O'Brian said. "Thanks for your help. We'll take it from here."

"This is a civil matter, Sergeant," Ichiro said. "I'm sure you understand that this goes beyond your jurisdiction."

"You can take that up with the base commander," O'Brian said. "We'll cooperate fully with civilian authorities."

"I'm not with the military!" Bolan said, and the AP on his left punched him hard in the ribs.

"Stop that!" Ichiro said, pushing past O'Brian to stand before Bolan. He opened Bolan's jacket enough to see the combat harness and then looked at the cut on his hand.

"We must go," O'Brian said, nodding toward the APs, who started to pull Bolan closer to the jeep. "We'll question him and send you a complete transcript."

"I'm a civilian," Bolan argued. "My passport's in my back pocket."

"Hold it a minute," Ichiro said, but O'Brian nodded to his men to continue.

"Stop now, or I'm placing you all under arrest!" Ichiro demanded, his face set rock solid. He walked up to Bolan and reached into his back pocket, pulling out the passport that Hal Brognola had obtained for him.

Bolan could hear sirens in the distance, coming closer fast. A small yellow fire engine skidded around the corner and pulled up in front of the demolished pachinko parlor.

O'Brian moved to within inches of Ichiro, but the Japanese lieutenant ignored him as he looked at the passport.

"We're taking him now," the AP said through clenched teeth. "Get out of the goddamned way."

Ichiro's leg flashed out quickly, his foot slamming O'Brian in the knee. The big man buckled like a penknife and dropped to the ground. The cop looked at the other two APs.

"You have fifteen seconds to pick that man up and get out of here—without your prisoner," he said coldly. They looked at each other for several long seconds as more emergency vehicles arrived. O'Brian, one hand on his knee, used the side of the jeep to try to struggle to his feet. "Now! And you can be sure that I will contact your CO to discuss this situation," Ichiro told them briskly.

Bolan broke from their grasp, his head starting to clear. He turned and made an effort to memorize his captors' name badges and faces. One was Jeffries, a

California blondie who looked as if he'd played football. The other was a tall black named Prine, who had a red scar on his left cheek.

They helped O'Brian to his feet and into the jeep. Bolan glanced around quickly, looking for an escape route, but four more police cars, along with ambulances, had arrived, and uniformed cops walked both sides of the streets. He'd never make it.

As Jeffries ground the jeep into gear, O'Brian, his face strained in pain, glared at Bolan. "You're meat," he said, pointing a stubby finger. "Both of you," O'Brian continued as he turned his icy gaze on Ichiro.

"Leave the weapons," Ichiro said. O'Brian tightened his lips and reached down to the floorboards to toss the Beretta and the AutoMag to the lieutenant one at a time.

The jeep slid off as confusion settled on Bolan again. What was that all about? Why had they been at the pachinko parlor to begin with, and why didn't they stop the leather boys? Bolan wondered.

Reality flooded back as Bolan felt the snap of a handcuff on his right wrist. Ichiro fixed the other cuff to his own left wrist. He stared up at Bolan with dark, unreadable eyes.

"Everyone wants you, Mr. Reeves," he said without inflection. "I've got you."

"Me and about a hundred yen will get you on the bullet train," Bolan said.

Ichiro looked at him hard. "Did you do this?" he asked, gesturing toward the demolished building.

"No," Bolan said firmly. "A bunch of punks riding motorcycles and dressed in black leather came in shooting and then left the bomb as a little going-away present."

"How do you explain your weapons?"

"It should be obvious that your streets are unsafe."

The man's face remained impassive. Only the corners of his mouth turned down for just a second to register his irritation. "The truth will get you a great deal further in this world, Mr. Reeves."

"What is truth, Lieutenant?" Bolan asked as the man walked him back toward the smoking ruins. The fire fighters were busy pouring water onto the small blaze; emergency workers were already digging through the rubble looking for bodies. The continual arrival and departure of ambulances assured Bolan that the wounded were being taken care of.

The street was filled with glass and fragments of wood. Loose ball bearings were still tripping people, and Bolan had to watch the ground to keep from slipping. He saw an arm somehow balanced atop a street sign; he saw a foot, still in its shoe, lying in the gutter. And he saw a hat, a red Phillies hat, and thought about an old man named Maruki who had known all about Operation Snowflake but had no idea what cocaine was. The old man's last words had been a plea for help, a plea that Bolan hadn't been able to respond to.

Ichiro called his people together and then directed Bolan into the back seat of the small police car. Two of Ichiro's men took the front to drive them away

The lieutenant turned to study his captive. He looked young, Bolan thought, but he knew that looks were often deceptive. His face was pleasant and unlined; a quick intelligence showed in his eyes. Bolan determined to take it easy with this one. He was smart—and no punk.

"I don't know who you are," Ichiro said to him, "or why those men wanted you so badly. But if you had anything to do with the tragedy here tonight, you will never leave my country again. Do you understand what I'm saying to you?"

Bolan nodded. "I didn't do it," he said again.

The other man nodded quickly. "I am taking you to see something before we go to the station."

Only the squawk of the radio broke the silence as they drove in the direction of the base. Bolan watched as electronics stores and gift and tailor shops slid by his window, their neon colors running together on the wet glass.

They reached Yokota's main gate within minutes, but a large-scale demonstration of some kind blocked off the entire six-lane street skirting the huge complex that had housed much of the Japanese Air Force during the Second World War.

"You can thank this crowd for your arrest," Ichiro said. "I arrived so quickly at the scene of the bombing because we were working crowd control."

The car pulled up to the fringes of the demonstration, and Ichiro dragged Bolan from the vehicle. "Up," he said, indicating the police car's roof.

The men, still handcuffed together, scrambled up onto the roof of the car, standing to get a good view of the demonstration. Several police vans stood on the outskirts of the crowd that Bolan estimated numbered one thousand.

"What's going on?" Bolan asked the cop.

"They protest." Ichiro shrugged. "Do you see anything that seems familiar to you?"

Bolan quickly scanned the crowd. It was dark, but the pole lights on the chain-link fence that walled off Yokota kept the area well lit. There were many people, young mostly, shaking their fists and pushing against the gate. They carried signs denouncing the American presence in their country and shouted many Japanese slogans in unison.

Then Bolan saw them, a group set apart from the rest, about thirty strong. They all wore black leather, with black helmets and a red circle over their hearts.

"There," Bolan said, pointing. "The ones who attacked the parlor were dressed like that."

Ichiro nodded. "They call themselves Sonnojoi, those who 'repel the barbarians and revere the Emperor' and we suspect that they're an offshoot of the Red Army, although we haven't been able to crack them yet. Unfortunately, they seem to generate violence wherever they go. Look."

He pointed. The leather boys had shoved their way through the chanting crowds up to the gate to within inches of a contingent of Air Police standing at parade rest on the other side with their billy clubs behind their backs. The black-clad youths began jeering at the APs, trying to make them lose their composure.

"What are they protesting?" Bolan asked.

"Americans," Ichiro said. "Your presence on our soil. The war was a long time ago. They think it's time for you to stop treating us like a conquered nation."

"And what do you think?"

"I am a policeman, Mr. Reeves. I just keep the peace."

The bikers produced several pairs of wire cutters and tried to cut through the gates. Others poked sticks through the mesh to keep the APs back.

Ichiro bent down and spoke quickly to the man with the radio in the front seat. He stood again.

"Now you'll see how I feel about lawlessness," he said.

As if on signal, the back of the police vans opened and riot police came pouring out, all of them wearing helmets with long visors. They carried large rattan shields, which covered most of their bodies, and long poles.

The squad waded into the crowd and began swinging their poles, aiming for shins. Bolan watched the targeted demonstrators clutch their legs. Shin pain was not physically damaging but nearly unbearable.

They moved quickly, dispersing most of the crowd in less than a minute. It was the most effective riot control Bolan had ever seen. When the riot police reached the leather boys, the bikers simply stopped what they were doing and darted off into the night, the same thing they had done at the pachinko parlor.

Bolan and Ichiro watched from the top of the car for a moment, then climbed down as the crowd had obviously decided to go. There was no use in going after the bikers. Dressed as they were, there was no way Bolan could ever make any kind of identification.

"I'm impressed," Bolan said.

Ichiro's face remained impassive. "Get back into the car," he said. "We'll take you to the hospital to tend to your wounds, then on to the Oneida Station House. You should try and sleep a little now while you can. You'll be up all night answering questions."

"I want a lawyer."

"You have no rights under Japanese law, Mr. Reeves. None."

Bolan knew he was very much on his own in this one.

3

The Japanese Zen Masters teach that life is pain, and only the acceptance of the inevitability of pain brings happiness. Mack Bolan must have been a very happy man indeed.

Bolan sat cross-legged on the floor of the dingy cell, his chopsticks clattering methodically against the rice bowl as he ate to maintain his strength. It was a small local jail with only six cells, but once Ichiro had finished running his prints and ID through Interpol, he knew he'd be moved to more prestigious surroundings.

The only question that remained at this point was whether they'd try to keep him in Japan or allow extradition to any one of the hundreds of countries in which he was an actively sought fugitive. The Executioner had been a very busy man.

Trained to fight in the jungles of Vietnam, he had returned to America to find his family dead, devastated by the loan sharks and pimps of the Mafia. Unable to get satisfaction through the courts, he had taken on the mob single-handedly, dispensing final justice in the same terms that had been dealt to his family. As he had learned more and more about the nature of evil that threatened the lives and security of the decent people of the world, Mack Bolan had expanded his fight to include terrorists. No matter what they called themselves, no matter what platitudes they used to justify their mayhem, Bolan knew they were all the same—mad dogs reveling in the kill, satisfying their sinister urges with warm, innocent blood.

Not everyone found the Executioner's cause, or the methods he used to further it, noble. Because he walked beyond the bureaucratic cage of the law, there were those who thought him lawless. He'd learned to live with that long ago, but it didn't stop him from hurting. It didn't stop the loneliness. But whenever he decided to back off, whenever he thought he'd had enough and done his share, there was always someone like the old man in the pachinko parlor to remind him that there was no one to take his place. So Toshu Maruki joined the long list of those Mack Bolan would avenge if he lived beyond the day.

And the Executioner had every intention of living. He lived to kill, not through desire but through necessity. He did the job that had to be done. He did his share to rid the world of evil. Hence the name the Executioner, the last bastion between civilization and the jungle. Life is pain.

Bolan finished his rice and stood, setting the bowl near the cell door. He wrapped his fingers around the cold bars, testing their strength. If he was to get out of there, it would have to be soon. Once they knew who he really was, the security would become a lot tighter.

He was feeling pretty good. They had cleaned and dressed his wounds at a local clinic, the worst gash requiring a couple of stitches in the palm of his left hand. Ichiro had been as good as his word and had kept him up all night for interrogation. Bolan had, of course, given nothing away, for there was nothing he could say that would have made any difference. He had absolutely no idea what had happened at the pachinko parlor; all he could have done was violate Hal Brognola's trust. Mack Bolan didn't operate that way.

Ichiro had impressed him in a positive way. It was unfortunate that they were on opposite sides of this problem. During the interrogation it was obvious that Bolan was frustrating the Japanese lieutenant by confessing so little information. The man was at all times polite and respectful, allowing Bolan the specter of innocence until he'd proven otherwise. But there was something else at work, as well. Ichiro had kept him awake to see if exhaustion would make the American's tongue any looser, and also to render him too tired to attempt escape.

With any other man it would have worked, but with Bolan adversity meant strength. He would tire, but he had learned to control it to the point that exhaustion could be channeled to a crystal-clear edge of awareness that made him even tougher. Mack Bolan had learned to make a lot out of very little.

The bars may have been old, but they were still solid. Bolan turned the other way. A small cot served as his bed. It had no pillow or covers. A privy and a sink took up one corner, but they had no hardware that could be disassembled and used. There were no windows. They had taken his torn and bloody clothes and given him an orange one-piece uniform to wear. His shoes had been replaced by the Japanese equivalent of Ho Chi Minh sandals. It was obvious that Ichiro had as much respect for him as he had for Ichiro. It made for tough opposition.

As if in response to his thoughts, he heard lone footsteps clicking down the hall toward the cell area. The pace was fast, and he knew from his own studies that Lieutenant Ichiro was coming to talk to him.

His senses became immediately alert. The man was alone, and if he could jump him, he might have a fighting chance at getting out of there. Bolan moved closer to the bars and waited.

He heard a door being unlocked, then the grating sound of the cell division bars sliding open. Within seconds he was staring into Ichiro's unreadable face. Bolan was not surprised to see that the all-night interrogation had had no visible effect on Ichiro, either.

"You leave me in a real dilemma, Mr. Bolan," he said.

"My name's Reeves," Bolan corrected.

Ichiro almost smiled. He was just out of arm's reach on the other side of the bars. Bolan moved a step closer; Ichiro stepped back a pace.

"Your identification is quite complete," the lieutenant said as he ran a hand through his closely cropped black hair. "And I'll have to say that I am aware of who and what you are."

"What happens now?"

The lieutenant pursed his lips. "That is a matter of some speculation. You see, other survivors of the bomb blast have confirmed your story about the presence of the Sonnojoi at the gambling house. So, from my perspective, you are not a suspect in this case. On the other hand, you are a wanted fugitive and you are traveling with a false passport and carrying concealed weapons in a country that strictly forbids such practices."

"Nobody's perfect," Bolan returned. "Can I have a cigarette?"

Mack Bolan rarely smoked, but he wanted the opportunity to get closer to the detective.

This time Ichiro did smile. "No, I think not, Mr. Bolan. After you are transferred, perhaps they will give you cigarettes, although I doubt that you would smoke them."

"Transferred to where?" Bolan asked.

"Hachioji Prison, a maximum-security facility."

Bolan had heard of the infamous Hachioji prison. People served their time there—all their time. It was not a holding cell. Few people lived to walk out through its doors.

The big man betrayed no emotion. Both he and his captor stared at one another. After a moment Ichiro asked, "Why have you come back to my country?"

"I can't tell you right now."

"You caused a great deal of havoc when you were here before."

"And saved a great deal."

"Yes," the lieutenant was forced to agree. "Were the Sonnojoi there to kill you?"

Bolan wrapped his hands around the bars, keeping the left one loose because of the stitches. Ichiro stepped out of his reach, and Bolan mentally put that particular game onto the back burner.

"I was quite honestly surprised to see them," he said. "I have no idea who or what they are."

"I believe you."

"You do?"

Ichiro nodded. "I do not feel that you've lied to me in any substantial matters yet. When you don't wish to answer my questions, you simply say so."

"I believe a man is only as good as his word," Bolan replied. "How come you speak such good English?"

"A cop in an Air Force town," he said. "Often as not, I'm the go-between in disputes that arise with the Air Force. We've always gotten along. That's why those goons from last night surprised me."

"And me, too," Bolan said. "They sat out there all through the attack."

Ichiro furrowed his brows. "Interesting," he said. "I spoke to their commanding officer again this morning, and he told me that the men had apologized profusely and admitted that they were overzealous in their attempts to subdue you. Having no jurisdiction on American soil, there was nowhere else for me to take the discussion."

"You told me before that I placed you in a dilemma," Bolan said. "What did you mean?"

"In my own way, Mr. Bolan, you and I are very similar," Ichiro answered. "I am the head of what we call Special Services, which is a clean way of saying a counterterrorist squad. As you know, since the Second World War, we have not been allowed to have a standing army. So our little military unit is an offshoot of the Tokyo Police Department. I headquarter here, between Yokota and Tachikowa Air Bases, where most of our problems seem to arise. You and your exploits are not unknown to me. And I have always had the utmost respect for what you do and for the constant pain you must live under." He bowed deeply, respectfully.

"But . . ." Bolan helped.

The man showed him empty palms. "But I have my own duty, and like you, it is my life. My duty right now is to see that you are kept locked away until such time as your case is handled through the proper channels. I admit to you that it is a sad duty but one that I would never shirk."

"I understand," Bolan said, and the two warriors locked eyes in mutual respect. Under other circumstances, the two men would have made a foreboding team. Now Ichiro could easily serve as the Executioner's executioner.

"I leave you now," Ichiro said. "I go to make arrangements for your transport to Hachioji. Should you want to talk about the events of last night either now or later, I will gladly make myself available."

"Are you married?" Bolan asked him.

The man nodded.

"Children?"

"I have two sons and a daughter."

"They must be proud of you," Bolan said. "You are a man of honor."

"I am a man of duty," Ichiro said. "That is not the same thing as honor. Perhaps you will find that out during your stay here."

And Bolan was left alone again.

Several hours passed in which the Executioner tried to solve the riddle of Operation Snowflake. He figured that another talk with his "friend" O'Brian, under better circumstances, might shed some light on the mystery. And then there was the matter of Dr. Norwood, whom Maruki had been so keen to protect. Who was he? Bolan wondered. How did he fit into the puzzle? Had those punks come to kill Maruki? And was the United States Air Force somehow connected with an anti-American group like the Sonnojoi?

There were questions but no answers as long as he remained in jail. Yet getting out of jail seemed nearly out of the question as long as Ichiro remained in charge. Bolan slept lightly for two hours, awakening to find they had brought him fish heads and rice for lunch.

He ate, although he had no desire to, and just as he was finishing, he heard the tramp of many feet and knew they were coming for him.

A contingent of six officers in crisp blue uniforms and white gloves escorted him from his cell. They handcuffed his hands behind him and put manacles on his legs. Bolan thought about trying to break free before they chained him, but with so many he couldn't have been sure of success without causing some degree of bloodshed.

He was surprised when Ichiro didn't show up in person to escort him out, but Bolan figured the lieutenant must have more things to do than guard one prisoner. They stopped at the booking cage on the way out, and after signing some papers, picked up the bagful of personal effects, including his guns.

He was taken out the back door and led toward a police van like the ones he had seen at the demonstration. Two men climbed in the back with him and ran the manacle chain through loops on the van's floor to hold him there securely.

When they drove off, the men in back with him were all smiles. They shook hands and slouched on the bench seats, smoking cigarettes. This didn't sit right with Bolan. There was something odd about the whole setup.

He tried to question them, but they apparently didn't understand English, so he just sat back and waited. They only drove for twenty minutes before stopping, and Bolan was sure by this time that something out of the ordinary was going on.

They opened the door to the van from the inside and hustled him out. He walked into bright sunlight in the middle of a residential neighborhood. They had pulled up in front of a house that sat by itself at the end of a cul-de-sac.

"What are you doing?" he asked.

"Please, sir," said one of the cops who he had thought couldn't speak English. "Come this way."

Bolan walked with the man, taking small steps because of the leg chains. They led him into the house after sliding open the wood-and-paper doorway that opened onto a living room. Only the cop carrying the bag with Bolan's personal effects came in with him.

The man unlocked Bolan's handcuffs, then gave him the key to the leg irons. As Bolan sat on a cushion to spring the lock, the man opened the bag and dumped everything on a table, including the Executioner's weapons and combat harness.

"Someone will come for you at seven o'clock," the man said.

"And what if I'm not here?"

The cop shrugged. "Do what you want," he said.

Bolan was confused. "What's going on?" he asked again.

The man just smiled and walked out of the house, sliding the door closed behind him.

Bolan quickly unlocked the manacles and leaned over to pick up his Beretta. It was loaded. He ran to the front door and slid it open. The street was empty, the police van was nowhere in sight.

4

Bolan sat cross-legged on the tatami floor and used his finger to push the small papier-mâché figurine that wobbled before him on the low Japanese table that was the only piece of furniture in the room. The figure represented a monk of some kind and had a rounded bottom so that, no matter how he pushed it, it returned to a standing position.

The toy had been waiting for him there at the house, and somehow he felt it had been meant as a gift. It, like everything else, made absolutely no sense.

Bolan looked at his watch. It was almost seven. He hadn't been back long. After being dropped off by the mysterious police—if that's what they were—he had gone through the bag containing his belongings and found his tattered clothes. He'd put on his trousers, then changed into a cotton *yukata* he'd found in the house. He was sure it had been meant for him.

The *tsuyu*, or plum rains, had been falling all day and he had been forced to wear a pair of wooden clogs to make his way through the muddy streets to try to find out where he was.

The house was protected by a tree-lined hairpin turn that was impossible to see unless one was looking for it. The neighborhood was blue collar, and probably all of its inhabitants worked for the same company. The houses were uniform and traditional—wood and paper. He had walked barely five blocks before running into the long stretch of chain-link fence that defined Yokota Air Base. He wasn't far from where he had started the night before, and for some reason that seemed appropriate.

He'd found a shop and purchased a tour book to try to find the place where the old man had told him he'd find Dr. Norwood, but Bolan couldn't find a listing for a place called Fujikyu, or for a Fujikyu Shrine. It was possible he'd misunderstood Maruki, but Mack Bolan was a man used to listening carefully, and he had committed the name to memory.

He'd thought about putting a call in to Hal Brognola, but he had nothing to relate to the man. Besides, with at least a fourteen-hour time difference it would be the middle of the night in D.C.

So Bolan, a man of action, was forced to play the waiting game. As he sat in the house of delicate rosewood and sliding paper walls, with the monsoon rains tapping on the wooden shingles, he couldn't help but feel that he had been drawn into the midst of a block puzzle, and that one missing piece provided the key to the construction of the whole framework. But he was playing the puzzle under someone else's rules, and the Executioner didn't like that. He knew that the secret to staying alive lay in controlling the situation. Bolan confused was Bolan in mortal danger. He'd wait—for now—but the weapon that was his body was tuned and ready, and he'd take the initiative at the very first opportunity.

He didn't have to wait long.

At precisely 7:00 p.m. a sleek Honda sports car roared up in front of the house. It was a model the Japanese didn't export to the United States. The car looked like a Porsche and, from the sound of the engine, was capable of the same road performance.

Bolan uncoiled his lanky frame easily, glancing down at the Beretta in his hand. He moved quickly through a sliding panel, then out the back of the house and around the side to view the front, his bare feet sinking into the wet ground. The rain had slowed to a drizzle.

A slim man in a dark suit with long hair got out of the car and walked easily up the stone walk to the door. Bolan came around behind him.

"Hold it right there," Bolan said in English, hoping the man would understand. "Hold your arms straight out from your body."

The man did as he was told, moving slowly without looking back. Bolan quickly backpedaled to the car and glanced in to make sure that the driver was alone.

"Turn around," he called. "Slowly."

The man turned, exposing a young, boyish face. A half smile was fixed on his lips.

"Back slowly into the house," Bolan said, and the man reached down to take off his shoes. "Move."

The man shrugged and did as he was told. Bolan followed him into the house.

"You understand English?" the Executioner asked.

The man smiled again, nodding.

"Good," Bolan said. "Take your jacket off and drop it on the floor."

The man removed the sports jacket and dropped it. As Bolan kicked it away, he looked at the man and said, "I'm going to pat you down for weapons. Stand facing the door, hands on it."

The man assumed the defenseless position, and Bolan kicked his legs back farther. Bolan sided his weapon and began frisking the silent driver, immediately making a strange discovery.

The woman did nothing to show that she knew she'd been found out. Bolan finished the search, turning up nothing, then spun the woman around to face him.

"Who the hell are you?" he asked.

"My name is Junko Hashimoto," she said in a soft, feminine voice that didn't match her mannish clothes. "My esteemed father, Inazo Hashimoto, sends his greetings to the famous Mack Bolan." She bowed deeply.

Bolan picked her jacket up off the ground and handed it back after checking it. "What's going on here?" he demanded.

She ignored his question and walked over to the table, picking up the figure. "I see you have found the *Daruma*, our present to you."

"What does it mean?"

She looked at him with deep dark eyes. "It is the representation of a Zen monk who sat so long in meditation that his legs withered away. It never falls over, representing recovery from misfortune. We are your friends, Mr. Bolan. You need not fear us."

Bolan felt himself relaxing somewhat, falling into the ease of the young woman's conversation. "I have many questions," he said.

"Just so," she said, bowing slightly. "And they will all be answered."

"Then—"

She held up a hand to silence him. "By my father. Will you go for a drive with me?"

He looked deeply into her eyes, but they were as unreadable as Ichiro's had been. He took out the Beretta but did not point it at the woman. "I'm not going anywhere until I know what this is all about," he said. "And you have about five seconds to tell me."

She smiled again. "You will not shoot me with your gun, I think," she replied simply, then lowered her eyes.

Bolan waited. He sided the 93-R. "Let's go for a drive."

She handled the machine like an expert, moving them along the Higashi Highway at a steady 90 clicks per hour despite heavy rush-hour traffic.

To their left, the mammoth fairyland of steel and glass known as Tokyo sprawled in all directions, and where it couldn't grow out, it grew up. It was a totally modern city in every sense of the word, built on the ruins of its predecessor, Edo.

"Can you tell me where you're taking me?" he asked, turning to look behind them. His acute senses were on edge. A warning flashed in his mind.

She smiled over at him. "The Ginza," she said. "I think my father wants to impress you."

"And can you tell me why you're dressed like a man?"

"I have a destiny to fulfill," she said without elaborating.

The hairs were standing up on the back of Bolan's neck. He half turned in the seat, catching a swath of black as it swerved behind a Sapporo Beer truck.

"Change lanes," he said.

"Why?"

"Just do it."

She put her foot on the gas, outrunning a car beside them and then cutting in front of it. For a few seconds he got a clear view of him, a Sonnojoi on a motorcycle, maneuvering to get closer.

"Trouble," he said. "We're being followed."

"Can't be."

And then Bolan saw the second one, two lanes over, nearly parallel with them. The leather boy's shotgun was strapped on his back. Bolan turned to look out the back window again and thought he saw a third a bit farther back in the quickly moving traffic.

"How good are you with this thing?" he asked, reaching up to crank open the sunroof.

"I've raced professionally," she said.

"Good," he replied. "You drive."

Bolan unholstered both automatics, setting the AutoMag on the console between them. He stood on the seat, poking his head and upper body through the sunroof. From there he had a good view of the road in every direction. Sonnojoi were carefully spaced around them. He turned a complete circle and counted six, two of them in front.

The Executioner felt his lips curl over his teeth. He didn't know what was going on, but he knew the enemy when he saw him. And he knew what to do.

He leaned back down into the car. Junko was slipping into racing gloves, her eyes intent on the road.

"It may get rough!" he yelled.

She shot him a glance, then nodded, her jaw set. Bolan hated to put her in such a critical spot, but he had no other choice. The Sonnojoi were tightening the noose, closing in on them from all sides.

The road turned into a long, looping overpass that rose high into the air above Tokyo's slums. It was as if a planner thought the height would insulate the drivers from the misery.

The motorcycles closed in at once. As Bolan turned to his left; the punk in the black helmet beside them was unslinging his Remington.

The cycle veered closer, the man steering with his left hand as he swung the rifle around with his right. Bolan didn't wait for an introduction. Bracing his arm on the roof, he aimed for the punk's head. The shot merely nicked the helmet, but it jerked the man enough so that he got his shot off too quickly. The passenger's window of the Porsche clone shattered into a million pieces.

Junko yelled once but didn't lose the road, as Bolan put another shot into the helmet. This time brains splattered out the other side, and the motorcycle veered sharply to the right, crossing in front of a car.

It hit the overpass rail, and the punk's body flipped over the handlebars to fall sixty meters to the roof of a dwelling below.

"Bolan!" Junko yelled. "Front!"

He turned just in time to see one of the motorcyclists take aim at them. No time to sight, Bolan tracked and fired from instinct. The man's spine exploded. He came up off the bike, his body hitting the hood of their car and rolling to the windshield. His cycle jagged left, where the oncoming car hit it and spun, causing other cars to pile up.

"I can't see!" Junko screamed, and Bolan dropped the Beretta back into the car and leaned down to try to dislodge the body from the hood, where it was bleeding all over the windshield.

Another punk came up beside Bolan as he leaned over the front of the car. Junko jerked right, and the man's shot went wild as he steered to avoid them. Unable to pump, he bumped up close, using the shotgun as a bludgeon.

Bolan was vulnerable, stretched out with two hands on the dead punk as Junko veered wildly across the road. The punk swung out hard, and a wave of excruciating pain shot through the big man's ribs.

He gritted his teeth and screamed into the wind, pulling the body off the car and literally tossing it onto the motorcycle beside them. Bike and rider went down in a tangle of limbs. The beer truck bounced hard over the debris and jackknifed, smearing the leather boy all over the parkway as its trailer twisted off the mooring to slide to a horrible screeching crash. Thousands of bottles of beer burst from its seams to cover the road in a cascade of glass and foam. Cars swerved and skidded, tires shredding on the glass as they piled into one another, blocking the highway completely from behind.

Bolan let himself fall back through the sunroof, wrapping his arm around his side as the pain shot through him. Junko was glued to the wheel, staring past the wipers that worked to clear away the blood. Bolan reached for the AutoMag as one of the leather boys drove quickly up on his side, gunning his engine.

Bolan kicked his door open and the punk drove right into it, taking it off the hinges. He flew over the handlebars and came down on his neck, head and helmet separating from his body to bounce crazily down the highway.

Bolan had counted four. Two left. Another had dropped back and was holding his shotgun stiffly.

"Down!" Bolan shouted, pulling Junko over with him as the windshield blew out in a shower of glass. They sat up quickly, Bolan emptying the AutoMag into the biker as Junko crossed two lanes of traffic to go after the last motorcyclist on her side of the car.

The man saw her coming, but he lost his shotgun as he grabbed the handlebars with both hands for control. He slowed, trying to drop back, but Junko geared down, moving into his lane and shoving him over.

She moved him closer and closer to the guardrail. When the punk increased speed, so did Junko, edging ever closer. There were only inches between them and inches separating the punk from a sheer drop to the ground below. They could hear him yelling hysterically. It was some of the best driving Bolan had ever seen.

He caught her eyes for just a second, and he saw something wild, something irrational, in them. Then she moved the wheel just a touch. The man, caught between the rail and the car, twisted off the bike and over the rail. He reached downtown Tokyo the quick way.

Bolan breathed out, easing himself down in the seat. "You aren't bad," he said.

She smiled over at him, hurrying to join the flow of traffic in front of them. "You're not so bad yourself," she said in a light but firm voice, before beginning to pull her gloves off with her teeth.

Bolan pulled the clip out of the AutoMag, throwing it out the open door to bounce along the highway. He reached inside his *yukata* to grab another from his combat harness. What in the hell had he gotten himself into? he wondered.

5

Lieutenant Ichiro walked along the blocked-off stretch of the overpass surveying the damage. He carried a bright red umbrella, the rain pattering gently against it. Nearly a kilometer of road was blanketed with human and metal debris. Everywhere the beam of his flashlight fell was more devastation.

Though they had opened up one lane to slow-moving traffic, the jam caused by the pileups stretched back over five miles. The darkness of the night was punctuated by a continuous string of headlights and the silence by blowing horns.

Emergency vehicles and city cleanup crews worked all around him. The beer truck driver jumped up and down, yelling, as a street crew swept up the remnants of his entire load. The roadway smelled like a brewery.

He walked to the edge of the drop-off, where a motorcycle was still twisted around a guardrail as if it belonged there. The driver's body was illuminated below by the lights of the ambulance that was there to take him away.

Sonnojoi.

And the Executioner was loose on the streets.

"Lieutenant," came a voice behind him, and he turned to see his assistant, Sergeant Natsume, who was wearing a bright yellow slicker and rain hat.

Hands on the guardrail, he returned his gaze to the city street far below as the ambulance drivers picked up the sheet-covered body and placed it in the back of their van. "What have you got, Yukio?"

"The final count is six dead," the sergeant said as he wiped the rain off his face.

Ichiro turned to him. "Sonnojoi?"

"All of them."

"Hai." Ichiro resumed his walk, letting the flashlight beam sweep easily along the roadway. Natsume walked with him. "What else?"

"Twenty-seven cars involved in the pileup with the beer truck, a few minor injuries, bumps and bruises."

"Did anyone see anything?"

"It happened too fast," Natsume said. "The truck driver gave us the best description. He said the men on motorcycles all had shotguns and that they came upon a crazy American who poked his head out of a sunroof and blasted them away."

Ichiro suppressed a smile. Bolan. It had to be. "Anything else on the breakout today?"

Natsume wiped his face again. "They found the van abandoned in a rice field a little while ago. They're examining it now."

The flashlight caught something glittering on the road. Ichiro moved toward it, stooping. "They won't find anything," he said.

He handed Natsume his umbrella and pulled a pen from inside his sports jacket. He stuck the pen in the middle of the metal object on the ground and picked it up, examining it under the flashlight. The expended clip of an automatic pistol.

He stood and handed Natsume both the clip and pen, taking back the umbrella. "Have them dust this and also that section of car door we found for fingerprints," he said. "Then try and match them to the prints we took from the man who broke jail today."

"Hai," Natsume bowed quickly and hurried off.

Ichiro stood at the end of the long line of destruction and turned back to stare at it, shaking his head. How could one man cause so much mayhem?

There was absolutely no doubt in his mind that Mack Bolan had been involved in the melee here today, though how he had managed to get out of jail was still a mystery. He respected the man tremendously, was secretly happy to see so many dead punks. He had suspected for quite some time that the Sonnojoi were involved with racketeering—especially drug running—to finance their hate campaigns, yet the constraints of the law kept him from going after them the way he'd like to do. But this—this was too much. Innocent people could have been hurt. No, as much as he liked and respected Bolan, he'd have to track him down and bring him back to face the consequences of his actions. And Kendo Ichiro rarely failed to bring in a suspect.

THE FRENCH RESTAURANT atop the Sony Building was very dark, save for a few candles that burned on the table of Bolan's host, Inazo Hashimoto, or Hashi-san, as everyone seemed to call him.

Mack Bolan stood before the floor-to-ceiling window that stretched across the whole side of the restaurant and looked down at the glitter of the Ginza.

The city was like a giant child's toy, all bright reds and yellows, flashing neons and huge movie billboards. This was where everyone, native and visitor alike, came to play. The Ginza. The Street. Shops and restaurants and theaters jammed together along wide sidewalks that were built to accommodate thousands of people at a time. Across from him a giant, computer-controlled billboard lit the sky, its flickering lights pantomiming men playing basketball while advertising a soft drink.

"They call you Striker," Hashi-san called to him from the table.

"Sometimes," Bolan said, turning to stare at the man.

There were three people seated at the table. Hashimoto, a small, unremarkable man with wire-rimmed glasses, Junko, who had changed into a beautiful white silk kimono complete with a flower in her hair, and a strange, nondescript character in a black business suit they simply referred to as Dr. Mett. Mett was a quiet man of indeterminate origin, who seemed to be Hashimoto's bodyguard. Bolan couldn't place him in these surroundings and simply added him to the growing list of mysteries that were confronting him.

"How do you like my city?"

"It's a city," Bolan said, turning from the window and moving back to sit at the table. "You broke me out of jail?"

Hashi-san smiled with thin lips. "You are a man who gets to the heart of the matter," he said.

"And you're a man who doesn't like to answer questions."

The old man bowed and waited as a waiter moved quickly through the darkness to clear the dishes off the table before speaking. "Much of what you see out of that window belongs to me," he said. "Tokyo was destroyed by firebombs in 1945, a city of wood and paper. We were reborn into the age of the computer, and I helped to rebuild with glass and steel, especially with steel. My people call me Hashi-san, meaning 'the bridge,' because I try to bridge the gap between the old ways and the new, between the ancient Japanese spirit of *yamato damashii* and the realities of the present day."

"You speak English very well," Bolan said.

"Domo arigato," Hashimoto said, bowing again. "English is the international language of business, a language I must speak to survive, for my country to retain its greatness in the world."

"What has this got to do with me?" Bolan asked.

"Most everything, Mr. Bolan," Junko said.

"Maybe I'm a little slow," Bolan replied. "Why don't you explain it to me."

When the old man got up, Bolan realized how frail he was. He moved to the window and stood with his back to it, the glitter of Tokyo surrounding him.

"I helped rebuild my land after the war with the Allies," he said. "And I became very rich because of it. But as is the tradition of my people, business is only a means for me to take care of my family, a legacy to pass on to them.

"I had a son, Mr. Bolan, a fine young man who, I'm afraid, I indulged too much for his own good. He became involved in the buying and selling of illegal drugs, poisons to rot the minds of our heritage, our youth. By the time I found out, it was too late. He was killed by local criminals in a drug buy. His body was hacked up for a few thousand yen worth of white powder."

"Cocaine?" Bolan asked.

Hashi-san nodded slowly. "Cocaine." The old man drew a long breath. "Do you know what it's like to have your world destroyed before your very eyes?"

"Yes," Bolan answered quickly, his insides tightening involuntarily.

"I believe you do," Hashi-san said, walking over to sit next to Bolan. "Soseki was my only son. When he was gone, my reasons for being alive were gone, also. My world became empty. Junko, my daughter, has tried to fill her brother's shoes and I honor her for that, but . . ." A deep sadness overcame Hashi-san as he looked down at the table. He looked up, lips quivering. "She is not a man. My family name, my lineage, dies with me. I am a Buddhist, but my roots are Shinto. We worship our ancestors . . . but there will be no one to honor me."

Bolan thought of a young woman trying hard to be a man, and he thought about the drug traffic in Japan. "Did the Yakuza do it?"

"Yakuza, yes," Hashi-san said. "And others. Sonnojoi."

"You are the one who got me out of jail," Bolan said.

"Governments are run by business," Hashi-san said. "In Japan we make no game of it. I am made aware of everything that goes on in my city. When I heard of your arrest and the circumstances and your identity, I . . . arranged for you to be set free."

"Why?" Bolan asked.

"You have already saved my daughter's life tonight," he said, smiling.

"Junko is quite capable of taking care of herself," Bolan replied.

Junko bowed her head, flushing. "I—I am not worthy of such a compliment."

"Do you know what Bushido means?" Hashi-san asked.

The Executioner nodded. "The way of the warrior."

"Loyalty to one's master," Dr. Mett said, his voice without inflection or accent. "Defense of one's status and honor, fulfillment of all obligations."

"I will tell you the story of the forty-seven *ronin*, the masterless samurai," Hashi-san said. "And then you will understand all. In 1700 the original lord of the samurai, Asano, was taking a lesson in court etiquette in Tokugawa Castle, right here in Tokyo, when he was insulted by a government official. Asano, defending his honor, drew his sword and wounded the official, although this was contrary to strict laws controlling the use of weapons in the castle. As a result, he was obliged to commit suicide. His retainers dispersed, vowing revenge, which they accomplished two years later by killing the official. In turn, although their act of loyalty was approved, they were obliged to commit suicide, all forty-seven of them. These *ronin* are our national heroes, Mr. Bolan. Their code of honor, the Bushido, is my code. I am a direct descendant of Asano."

Bolan stood, looked down at the faces of Junko and Dr. Mett and remembered the look on Junko's face just before she rode the Sonnojoi biker over the edge of the overpass. He also thought about a conversation he'd had with Lieutenant Ichiro about honor. He took out his Beretta and Big Thunder and laid them on the table. "You want to avenge the death of your son," he said.

The old man picked up the guns and studied them, the gesture not lost on him. "I am sworn to uphold the honor of my family and my country," he said. "I *will* have my vengeance. This poison of cocaine is destroying the fabric of our youth. I will have an end to it, and perhaps my son will rest in peace. His dead face haunts me. Even in my sleep there is no escape." He looked up at Bolan, his eyes as old as eternity. "You understand me, don't you."

It wasn't a question but a statement, and in it Bolan found the measure of his respect for this man. "We are of a kind, Hashi-san," he said. He clenched a fist and held it out in front of him. "You and I, just like this. I also have known pain and anger. I also seek to quiet the faces that haunt me. Tell me what you want from me."

The old man stood also, bowing. "It is not what I want from you, but what I have to offer if you desire it, Striker." He gestured once again toward the window and the magnificent city that throbbed below. "I *am* Japan. I have unlimited resources at my disposal. I have a private force under the direction of Dr. Mett. We have isolated much of the operation that processes this powdered evil, and we will go in and kill . . . and destroy the evil once and for all. My resources are yours to command—if you want them. If not, we walk away from one another tonight, carrying with us mutual respect."

"I put my weapons on the table for you," Bolan said, and in that gesture the Executioner said everything. Hashi-san nodded.

Dr. Mett stood and moved around to Bolan, shaking his hand firmly. "I look forward to serving under you," the man said.

"And you," Bolan said, then turned to Hashi-san. "A question. Have your ever heard of Operation Snowflake?"

The old man looked puzzled and shook his head. "No," he said, then looked at Mett, who was also shaking his head. "Is this of importance?"

"I'm honestly not sure," Bolan replied. "Are you aware of any large-quantity drug sales involving U.S. military personnel?"

"The Air Force," Mett said and grunted. "Our contacts have led us to the Air Force many times."

Bolan moved to the table, picking up his weapons and putting them back in their harness. "I want to move on this as soon as possible," he said. "Also, I'm answerable to no one or nothing save my own conscience."

"I would expect no less," Hashi-san replied.

"One final thing," Bolan said, habit making him unable to bring himself to reveal too much of his own limited knowledge. "Someone once told me to visit Fujikyu when I was in Japan, but I've been unable to find it on any of the maps."

Junko was smiling widely. "That's because it's local slang," she said. "It is the term we apply to the trains that leave Shinjuku Station for Lake Yamanaka at Mount Fuji. There is the very popular Sengren Shrine there. It's quite beautiful.''

"Perhaps I'll go," Bolan said, and the first piece of the puzzle had fallen into place.

6

Captain Hank Jamison sat on the flight line in the jeep watching the loading of the KC-135 supertransport fifty yards away. The KC was one of the largest airplanes in the world and was able to transport close to one hundred tons of cargo. It was being loaded with steel crates stamped Radar Bay and earmarked for every U.S. air base in America. What the crates actually contained was enough cocaine to burn the brains out of several million people, enough cocaine for Hank Jamison to pay back the government for all the pain they'd caused him in the past twenty years— and to make him a megamillionaire in the bargain. Not a bad night's work for a grounded sky jockey.

They'd trained him to frag gooks in Nam, and that's just what he'd done. Then they'd told him he'd fragged the wrong ones. Hell, what difference did it make? One gook was the same as another. Well, Jamison wasn't a man to let grass grow under his feet. If he couldn't fly for the government, he'd make the government fly for him.

His men worked quickly in the moist night air. It wasn't raining, but rain was never very far away. He watched them using the hoist to fill the cargo bay from the back of the truck. The operation was crisp and precise—military to the core. Jamison ran a tight ship and was proud of his boys.

One of the men separated from the plane and drove a pickup truck across the wet pavement toward Jamison. He didn't recognize O'Brian until the man had pulled up next to him, facing the opposite way so that their driver's windows were nearly butted up against one another.

"Another five minutes," O'Brian said, saluting. "The loading is going according to schedule."

Jamison snapped off a salute in return. "What's left after this, Sergeant?"

"Just the big packages for Travis and Andrews," O'Brian said. "And we should start movement on them tomorrow evening at 2000 hours."

"Good. Has there been anything else on that big guy you tried to pick up last night?"

"My man at Oneida tells me he somehow broke out of that Jap jail and is presently on the loose."

Jamison spit out the window. He didn't like loose ends, and this one meant trouble. He wasn't about to let anything interfere with this last operation. "You keep your people working on it, Sergeant O'Brian," he said. "I want that man found, and I want him disposed of—whatever it takes. Do I make myself perfectly clear?"

"Yes, sir!"

"I'm holding you responsible. I want that man's balls on my desk the day after tomorrow at the latest, or I'll have yours instead. That's all."

O'Brian saluted and put the Chevy truck in gear, gunning off in the direction of the transport. Jamison reached into his flight jacket and pulled out a pipe and leather pouch. He bowled the pipe, tapping the residue onto the wet ground. Refilling it from the pouch, he stuck the pipe's stem between his teeth and lit it. Reeves was the big man's name, but if he was an Internal man, he probably went by something else. Whatever it was, Hank Jamison wasn't going to let him screw this one up. Too much was riding on it. If he got in his way, Jamison knew he'd handle it just like he'd handled the gooks in Nam.

He'd never come up against a problem that couldn't be handled by a bullet between the eyes.

BOLAN AND JUNKO SAT in the back of Hashi-san's limo watching the all-night drugstore. It was midnight Tokyo time, which put it at 10:00 a.m. in Washington. Bolan had used Department of Defense authorization codes to try to reach Hal Brognola and was now waiting for his turn at the satellite.

Junko sat close beside him, still dressed in the silk kimono, and the subtle odor of cherry blossoms drifted from her hair like a breath of spring. He liked this woman. She was strong and principled, yet it never seemed to get in the way of her femininity. Just like April Rose, just like his lost love.

"The last time I rode in a limo in Japan," he said, turning to stare at the three-story nightclub across the slick street, "I ended up trapped in it at the bottom of Tokyo Bay."

Junko's eyes twinkled in the dim lighting. "Well, at least you managed to escape," she said, and he smiled.

"I was saved by a naked pearl diver."

"A pearl diver," she repeated. "You travel with luck, just like the figure of the *Daruma* I gave you."

Bolan nodded. "I thought she was a mermaid."

"To save a sailor's life. Perhaps she was."

A group of Amegurazoku, Japanese dressed like American greasers complete with leather jackets, sunglasses and slicked-back hair, walked into the drugstore. The radio one of them carried played an Elvis Presley song.

Bolan looked at Junko, seeing no trace of the woman who had ended the life of the cheap punk on the highway earlier. She was sweet and innocent, even shy. "Does your father know what he's getting into?" he asked.

She closed her eyes for just a second. "My father is a forthright and dedicated man. He always knows what he's doing and always gets what he wants. My brother's death nearly killed Hashi-san. His vengeance has been well thought out and well planned. All we lacked was . . . you, Mack Bolan."

Bolan turned slightly in the seat to face her. "Is it difficult to be his daughter, to share his determination? Wouldn't you rather hold down a normal job, or be married with a family?''

"To the Japanese, family is everything. I love and honor my father. What he wants is my want, as well. When he feels pain, it is my pain. I also loved my brother a great deal.''

"I didn't mean to imply that you didn't,'' Bolan said, embarrassed at how his question had come out. He felt awkward around Junko. "You just seem so...torn by what you are and what you must do.''

"Torn...yes.'' Her eyes misted, but she set her face with determination. "I am lonely sometimes. I have no one to confide in. I am my father's crutch, and he needs me for that. But who is to be my crutch?''

"No boyfriend? No lover?''

"There has been no time.'' She leaned back in the seat, her face sad. "Besides, I know no one except for the people who work for my father. He would never approve of such an arrangement.''

"I've got a good ear,'' Bolan said, reaching out to pat her knee. The familiarity startled both of them, and they pulled in a touch. "If you need someone to talk to, feel free.''

"There,'' Junko said, pointing past him. Bolan turned to see the owner of the drugstore waving frantically from his front door.

"That's my call,'' Bolan said, opening the door and stepping into the drizzle. "If you want to go on, I can get a cab back to the house.''

"I'll wait," Junko said. "I think I'd like you to listen."

Bolan smiled. Smiles came easily around her. "Give me ten minutes."

The Executioner moved across the wide downtown Tokyo sidewalk and into the harsh glare of the store. The owner pointed him to the phone booth in the corner, and he walked past aisles filled with the latest in gadgets and medications. The teenage greasers were busy reading rack magazines while the women shopped for makeup.

He moved into the old wooden booth and picked up the heavy red phone. *"Moshi-moshi,"* he said into the receiver.

"Is this Mr. Reeves?" came a distant Japanese voice, overlaid with static.

"Yes, it is."

"Go ahead, please."

"Mack? Is that you?"

"Hal! Good to hear your voice. Are you secured?"

"As much as possible. You got something for me?"

"Rumblings," Bolan replied, cupping his hands around the mouthpiece to get as much privacy as possible. "There are some crazy things going on here. I want you to run some names through the computer for me."

"Shoot."

"Master Sergeant Tom O'Brian. Tech Sergeants Jeffries and Prine."

"Are they involved in the ring?"

"They're involved in almost killing me," Bolan said. "Check 'em."

"What else?"

"A few shots in the dark. Try this name: Inazo Hashimoto. He's a Japanese industrialist. Just see what you've got on him. Also see if you have anything on an organization called Sonnojoi."

"Anything else?"

"See if you have anything on a man named Dr. Norwood. My contact at Yokota was killed after giving me the name."

"You don't mean Lawrence Norwood, the Harvard researcher?"

"I don't know who I mean. Tell me about this guy."

"He's a nuclear scientist who did a great deal of work on the development of the neutron bomb, but then had a change of heart and turned pacifist. He went to Japan about a year ago to protest the presence of nuclear carriers off the Japanese coast and was never seen again."

There was a commotion at the door. A group of drunk GIs had come in. They were harassing the greasers, calling them "fags" and pushing them around a little. One of them looked incredibly familiar.

"Mack . . . did you hear what I said? Mack . . ."

"Yeah," Bolan said, his eyes riveted to the back of the man he had singled out. "Find out the details for me, would you?"

"This guy's a big security hole, Mack," Hal said, excitement in his voice. "If you've got something..."

"I'm not sure," Bolan said and watched as the black man turned in his direction. It was Prine, one of the APs who had been at the pachinko parlor. They were paying for cigarettes and getting ready to leave. "Gotta go, Hal. I'll try to get back to you tomorrow at this time."

"Do you know what you're doing, Striker?" Brognola asked.

"Yeah," Bolan said. "Getting ready to pay a visit to an old friend." He hung up the phone and stepped from the booth as the five airmen left the drugstore.

He followed them out. They all had the look of APs but weren't wearing identifying arm bands, which meant they were off duty. As they crossed the sidewalk, one of them spat on the trunk of the limo, then walked into the street and headed for the nightclub on the other side.

Bolan gave them a head start, then walked quickly to the car, opening the back door. Junko smiled sweetly at him. "Got to see a man about a dog," he said. "You just go on home and get some rest."

"What's wrong?" she asked.

He thought about making up a story but knew instinctively that she wouldn't buy it. "Those men—" he indicated the APs "—were involved with the pachinko bombing last night. I'm going to have a little chat with them."

She started out of the car. "I'll help—"

"No—" he put out a hand to hold her back "—this one's my fight. I'll take care of it my own way. I'll call you tomorrow."

She lowered her head. "As you wish."

"I'll be in touch," he said and walked quickly away from the car.

"Be careful," she called after him, and he nodded.

He started across the wide street just as the airmen disappeared into the club. The place was called La Bomba and seemed to be all glass. Three floors' worth of young Japanese with Western tendencies drank and danced. A spiral staircase wound up the center of the building to the fourth floor. Bolan could not see through the opaque glass of the top story.

Bolan made the street, feeling strange, still wearing the robe, which was too short for him, that he had found at his "safe" house. He moved into the smoky bar where American jazz, heavy on the bass, throbbed through the semilit rooms. He was tensed for the kill. This was his first chance to meet his problems head-on, on his own terms, and he wasn't going to pass it up. Prine, the AP, was just as guilty as the punks who had lobbed the explosives into the gaming house, and the man was going to learn the meaning of instant karma.

There was a smattering of GIs with Japanese women seated about the room. First of the month, payday. Bolan moved slowly around the place but didn't see Prine's group anywhere. He had just started up the stairs to the second floor when he felt a hand on his arm. He turned, putting a casual smile on his face.

A large bouncer with a crew cut began talking to him in Japanese. He knew the guy was trying to tell him there was a cover charge, but he just played dumb, saying he didn't understand Japanese, and continued up the stairs.

The second floor was like the first. Women dressed in tuxlike outfits with fishnet hose moved around the tables, serving drinks in tall, frosted glasses. Still Bolan didn't see Prine. As he approached the stairs, the bouncer once again confronted him. This time a small man with a mustache stood beside the hulk.

"Hello," Bolan said. "Nice place."

"I'm sorry, sir," the man said, "but there is a cover charge to attend this club."

Bolan nodded broadly. "Oh, I understand. I'm not going to attend your club. I just want to find a friend of mine, then I'll go."

The bouncer and the little man talked for a moment, then the little man addressed Bolan. "We will find your friend for you," he said in halting English. "You wait downstairs by front door."

"Thank you," Bolan said, "but that's not necessary. I'll just wander around . . . it will be quicker."

Bolan made for the stairs, but the bouncer grabbed him. Bolan swung around and stepped hard on the man's foot, doubling him over. "Oh, I'm sorry," he said. "How clumsy. Here, let me help you."

He moved up to the off-balance man and nudged him slightly. The man toppled heavily upon a nearby table that crashed loudly to the floor as drinks and patrons scattered.

Bolan looked at the little man. "Sorry." He shrugged and hurried up to level three.

He had to haul it at this point. There'd be others to take the place of the bouncer soon enough. Somehow he wasn't surprised when he didn't find Prine up there, either. A guy like him would have access to that closed-off wing above.

The stairs ended at the third floor, and an elevator with an up arrow sat against the wall in its place. A man stood solemnly guarding the elevator. He was a lot bigger and a lot meaner-looking than the one Bolan had "helped" downstairs. It was getting thicker, and the Executioner liked that just fine.

He could hear angry voices downstairs as he moved toward the elevator. The man guarding it rose to meet him, and Bolan decided that the subtle approach wouldn't work anymore. Instead, he charged the man and slammed him hard into the wall behind.

The guard grunted loudly, and Bolan heard the air wheeze out of him. He slid to the ground, gagging, and was going into his jacket when the Executioner kicked out. Bolan's booted toe connected with the man's jaw in a loud cracking sound.

The man keeled over, unconscious, and Bolan pulled the Colt Python out of the guard's leather shoulder holster and ejected the clip.

The Executioner pushed the button, and the elevator doors slid open. He walked inside and smiled back at the customers who stared at him in wide-eyed wonder. He pressed the fourth-floor button and began flicking slugs out of the Colt's clip to clatter to the floor at his feet.

The Executioner was all movement when the doors slid open on four. Tightening his right hand around the empty clip, he walked quickly into the noise.

He was in a serious gambling establishment, where dark-suited men lorded over green-felt tables. The smell of hashish was thick like a cheap perfume. Two men moved up on him immediately.

"You can't—" the first one said, but Bolan silenced him with a hard right that moved his nose across his face and lifted him up off the ground, blood spurting from the busted cartilage.

The other didn't waste words. The bouncer grabbed and squeezed Bolan in a bear hug from behind. The Executioner loosened his muscles, giving the man his way, then tensed and threw his head backward, hard into the man's face.

The man yelled and released Bolan, who turned and shoved the off-balance thug back into the elevator, doubling him over with a knee to the groin and finishing the job with a right-fisted haymaker. The goon went down like wet cement, and Bolan pushed the button to send him back downstairs.

People were yelling and grabbing their own and everybody else's winnings off the tables. Confusion filled the crowded room, and that's what Bolan had hoped for. He moved into the crowd, searching for Prine. A hand flashed out for him, but he grabbed it and pulled, doubling it over his upraised knee until he heard the elbow joint snap. And then Bolan heard muffled screaming.

He moved toward the sound, finding a hallway with a series of numbered doors. Private rooms. They did it all here. In a genteel society like Japan's, the vipers would still have their way. They'd act sophisticated but still dirty the word "human" with their slime.

He threw off his robe, revealing a black kevlar shirt and combat harness, and filled his hand with Big Thunder. The men on the other side of that door wore the proud uniform of the United States Air Force. He respected the uniform and wanted to respect the men who wore it, but Bolan knew that creeps come in all shapes and sizes . . . and uniforms.

He kicked out at the door, the flimsy wood tearing at the hinges, and as Mack Bolan entered, the Bushido code flashed through mind.

He took in the situation with a glance. A large bed filled the center of the room. A Japanese teenager lay naked, spread-eagled upon it. Her face and body were cut and bleeding. Two of the APs held her down while Prine knelt between her legs, working at the belt of his pants. The other two airmen were knocking a second girl around, ripping her clothes off. A Japanese man stood off to the side with a large plastic bag full of white powder. It looked as if these girls had been kidnapped off the street and sold for pleasure to Prine and his buddies, and the payoff had been cocaine. Bolan knew that the ultimate fate of the girls would likely be slashed throats in a Ginza back alley.

Animals. Rabid animals.

Bolan had scoped the action the second he had jumped through the door. In the next second the animals reacted.

The Japanese showed his weapon first, and Bolan diced him twice in the chest, the AutoMag's .44 mm payload resounding in the closed-in room, sending the kidnapper into a whirling dance that dropped him onto the bed.

One of the APs holding Prine's girl was just clearing leather with his .45 when Big Thunder coughed in his face. His left eye became a blood-spewing fountain as he careened backward, crashing through the window to fall to the pavement below.

They were all on him then, charging, one of them pushing the half-clothed teenager in front of him. Bolan moved instinctively, but he didn't want to hit the girls or Prine, not until he got what he wanted. He dove forward and rolled, taking the legs out from under one of them, then burying the AutoMag in the man's gut and pulling the trigger. Viscera exploded— the man was a human piñata.

Everyone fell on him, a writhing mass of Air Force blue and screaming girls. Big Thunder was kicked from Bolan's hand as he tried to scramble out from under the biting, kicking pile.

He got partway free, when a .45 exploded beside his head, sending mattress stuffing throughout the room like snow. He snared the hand, turning it as the gun fired again, one of the animals screaming from within the pile.

The naked girl broke free and staggered to her feet, and Bolan kicked loose. He jumped up, shoving the girl toward the doorway and freedom as Prine pulled him back to the floor. Bolan came down on the man's chest, planting an elbow hard in his mouth, cracking his teeth in a bloody froth.

Another man was up, stumbling away, blood oozing thickly from his right thigh where a close-range blast from a service revolver had entered. He fell to the floor, screaming, grabbing his leg.

The remaining unscathed airman kicked Bolan hard in the back. The man jumped Bolan then, beating him with heavy fists. A blow to the back of the neck shot fire through Bolan's brain. With an effort he twisted hard, throwing the man off before falling on top of him.

The AP had a snarling, ugly face. Bolan punched him again and again until the AP's eyes were glassy, and then he got up slowly, dragging the man to his feet. He ran the man toward the smashed-out glass panel and pushed him in to the night.

He turned. Prine was trying to rise from the wood floor. He held his hand to his mouth as he coughed up blood. Bolan saw Big Thunder and grabbed for it, staggering back to the AP who had tried to kill him the night before.

The front of the man's uniform was soaked with blood. Bolan grabbed him, popping buttons, and pulled him to a kneeling position, jamming the gun into his throat, which made the man gag more.

The other girl was rising tentatively from the floor. Bolan looked at her. "Get the hell out of here!" he growled and turned back to Prine. "We're going to talk now."

"Go to hell," the man rasped, and when Bolan kicked him hard in the stomach, the man rolled into a fetal position on the ground.

Bolan pulled Prine back to his knees. "You're dead where you kneel," the Executioner said. "And don't think I don't mean it."

The man looked into his eyes and saw blue steel. He nodded slightly, his mouth a twisted mess. "What . . . ?" he asked weakly.

"Why were you at the pachinko parlor?"

The man's eyes drifted. Bolan shook him back.

"To make sure no Americans got out," he mumbled.

"Why?"

"P-part of the deal with our c-coke connection."

"Why?" he yelled.

He shook his head. "I don't know."

Bolan shook him hard. "Why?" he yelled.

"I swear to God, I don't know. We had to do it to get the coke."

"How much coke?"

"Tons . . . for distribution all over America . . . more than anybody's ever seen."

"Has it gone out yet?"

"No, man. N-no."

"Is this Operation Snowflake?"

"How did you . . . Yeah, that's it."

"Where is it? Right now, where is it?"

The man's lips quivered, and Bolan could see him still looking for a way out. The Executioner jammed the gun harder into his windpipe.

"Chikatetsu," Prine said, choking, spitting up. *"Chikatetsu."*

Bolan looked at him in disbelief. *Chikatetsu* was the Japanese word for underground, the term applied to the Tokyo subway system. That didn't make any sense, it . . .

He heard the gun being primed and rolled away instinctively, coming up to see Junko standing in the doorway with a MAC-10 in her hand. The wounded airman on the other side of the room had pulled a .45 and was swinging it away from Bolan toward Junko.

In a flash she opened up on full auto, cutting the man practically in half, his lungs exploding in fury from his chest cavity.

"Junko!" Bolan called as she swung the SMG across the room toward Prine, who was pulling his own .45 from its holster. "No!"

She fired as he cleared leather, drawing a line that bisected the AP from groin to head. His brains blew out the top of his head to splatter the walls. His body, dead already, remained kneeling for several seconds, then pitched forward with a loud splat onto the floor. The .45 was still locked tightly in his hand.

Bolan and the woman looked at one another, a slight smile turning up the corners of her lips.

"I thought I told you to go home," he said.

"And I thought I told you to be careful," she replied and pulled the clip from the automatic, rooting through her sequined handbag for another.

7

As Bolan stood looking across a sea of black hair, he understood why Junko had told him to wear white if he was taking the Fujikyu trip. The Shinjuku train was filled to overflowing with standing Japanese, head and shoulders smaller than Bolan and all wearing white for the climb up Mount Fuji. The climb is a metaphysical journey for the Japanese—Fujiyama's snowcapped peak is the home of their ancestral gods. And the climb itself is a Buddhist journey of self-discipline and physical purification.

The train rumbled toward Fujiyoshida Station, and the chatter around Bolan became more excited. The Executioner wouldn't be climbing all the way to the top of the long-silent volcano that he knew was the national symbol of Japan, but he welcomed some time in the clean morning air and the chance to reflect on the mysterious Dr. Norwood and Operation Snowflake.

Bolan felt the slowing of the old express train and bent with the other travelers to get a look out the train's windows at Fuji-san as they lumbered into the old wooden station. He hung back, waiting until the train had cleared before exiting himself. Bolan hated the Asian necessity for jamming as many people into as small a space as possible.

The air was crisp and still chilly as he made his way out of the station, following the crowd of climbers with their straw-covered shoes toward the Yoshida path, one of five hiking trails up the volcano. The sky was clear, crystalline blue, in stark contrast to the bright white of the snow-covered peak. To his left Lake Yamanaka, the largest of Fuji's numerous lakes, sat placidly. The whole atmosphere suggested peace and serenity.

The Executioner felt out of place.

He made the twenty-minute walk to Yoshida with a large group of climbers, most of whom intended to stay overnight and finish the climb before morning in order to see the sunrise at the summit—one of the most beautiful sights in the world. For not the first time in his life, Bolan felt the pull between duty and desire, but his own wants came second again. This was business; he'd given up pleasure years ago.

They reached the magnificent simplicity of the Fuji Sengen Shrine in short order, its sculpted wood rising from the shallows of Yamanaka. The climbers stopped here for a few minutes' rest before beginning the nine-hour ascent to the summit. Bolan went on. Time was of the essence.

A number of small chalets were set into the hillside several hundred yards from the shrine. Bolan moved toward them, hoping he'd find answers there. He knew that Fuji was an ancient Ainu word meaning fire, a not inappropriate hiding place for Dr. Norwood, a man who'd built his life around the modern fire of nuclear energy.

There were five houses within easy walking distance, and Bolan made a perfunctory stroll past each one. Children played beside one, and he ruled it out immediately. Of the other four, three were clearly inhabited. Only the fourth was closed tightly. It wasn't much, but it was the place to start.

He walked to the door of the wooden structure. It sat near the edge of an immense forest. Behind it the land rose sharply and climbed thirty-eight hundred meters to the summit of Fuji. The windows were shuttered tight.

He knocked lightly, then harder when no one answered the door. He reached into the pocket of his white jumpsuit and pulled out his picks, using one on the old lock. The door creaked open as he pushed it.

"Ohayo gozaimasu!" he called into the house, stepping onto the threshold. "Good morning!"

No response. He walked into the place, closing and locking the door behind him. It was warm in there, and the smell of rice and fish was strong in the air. "Hello!" he called again and moved carefully through the house, the 93-R never more than a second away from his hand.

A half-eaten plate of food sat on the kitchen table. Someone had left in a hurry. He moved to the kitchen window, and even though it was shuttered, the view through the slats commanded the entire shrine area and the ground between the two places. Bolan knew he'd been seen.

This time he took out the Beretta and searched the house carefully. A man, perhaps two men, lived there. Judging from the kind of books scattered around, the man was a scholar, and most probably a scientist. There was no doubt in Bolan's mind that it was Norwood, but where was he?

He went through the bedroom, finding a bag that still contained clothes—a man on the run. A *futon* with one pair of slippers next to it was set up on the floor. Next to the slippers Bolan saw something odd. A box of some kind, with an attached gauge.

He bent and picked up the gauge, recognizing it immediately as a Geiger counter. He flipped on the power and charge toggles, and the instrument sprang to life. The needle clicked wildly, fluctuating all over the dial.

The charged measuring rod was attached to the machine. He snapped it off and began taking readings. Bolan didn't know anything about radiation, but he knew a counter reading in the danger zone wasn't a good sign. The house was hot. It was hot as hell.

An involuntary chill ran up his spine, the fear of the unseen, and he bent to measure the dosage on the *futon*. The needle hit the upper end of the dial and stayed there as if it was glued. It wasn't the house that was hot. It was Norwood himself.

Bolan walked quickly through the place, taking readings. Every place where a person would spend any amount of time was hot; even the half-eaten food on the table was radioactive.

Bolan set the counter down and moved back through the place again, looking out the windows. Whoever had seen him—couldn't come down the mountain without Bolan seeing him. Norwood probably went farther up the slope or into the forest. If he had opted for the forest, he could stay hidden forever. But if he had climbed, Bolan would find him.

The long living room looked out onto the slope. The Executioner stationed himself there and peeked through the slats. If somebody was out there waiting, he'd show himself eventually.

Twenty minutes later he did. A hundred yards up the slope, hiding behind a small rise, Bolan spotted a man watching the house. He would poke his head up occasionally, then duck again. Bolan could simply wait him out, but he was betting on being in a lot better shape than a scientist who was suffering from radiation poisoning. Besides, Mack Bolan was not a man who waited around.

Bolan threw the door open and charged the slope, angling himself to make sure he got between Norwood and the forest. Everything else was in the open. He ran hard. The ground, soft from the rains, was slippery underfoot. Fifteen seconds after Bolan had exposed his position, Norwood was up and running.

The man had started running toward the forest, then stopped when he realized that Bolan could intercept him. He changed direction, losing valuable time, and hurried farther up the slope.

After that it was no contest. Within two minutes Bolan had caught him, grabbing the man and pulling him gently to the ground, both of them breathing hard.

"I'm not here to hurt you," Bolan said, looking at the man's frightened eyes. "I'm here to help."

Norwood was obviously sick. His skin was gray, his eyes sunken into dark pools. His hair was thin and what was left was almost pure white. Bolan knew he was much younger than he looked.

"Like you helped Toshu?" he asked loudly, and Bolan noticed that a large number of blood vessels had broken in the man's eyes.

"If you had told us more, we could have offered you more help," Bolan said, then softened his approach. "If I wanted to hurt you, I would have done so already. Let's go back down to the house and talk."

Norwood looked at him for a moment, then sighed in resignation. "Not the house," he said. "It's dangerous there for you. This hasn't worked out well at all."

"How sick are you?"

"I'm dying...rapidly." Norwood sat up on the hillside, looking at the mud patches on his clothes. He seemed overwhelmed by his lot in life. "Everything got so out of control, so crazy, Mr....Mr....?"

"Reeves," Bolan said. "What happened exactly?"

Bolan sat beside the man, staring down at the house two hundred yards below. There was some movement down there, but it could easily have been the occupants of the other houses.

The man ran his hands through his patchy, unkempt hair. "I—I'm not sure of anything," he said. "I'd worked for the government in fission development for nearly thirty years...and then something happened. I don't know, maybe it was the Chernobyl incident in Russia, but I suddenly felt that nuclear power was not in the best interests of the world. It's a matter of the idea of progress being inherently good. I'd always believed that technology was good, but then I began to think that we were simply advancing our own destruction. I—"

The man doubled over coughing loudly, blood coming up with the spit. Bolan reached out to help Norwood, but he pulled away. "Don't contaminate yourself," Norwood said.

"How did you come to Japan?" Bolan asked.

"I'd written a paper." Norwood wiped his mouth on his sleeve and laughed dryly. "A high-school thing to do, but I wanted everyone to know how I felt. It was published in several places and denounced nuclear energy. Then I got a phone call from a gentleman in Japan, who told me that many people here felt as I did, and he invited me to take part in a symposium concerning nuclear energy in Tokyo. I accepted."

Bolan looked down the hill, a line of worry creasing his forehead. Several figures seemed to be moving directly toward Norwood's house while others went to the other homes.

"We might need to move away from here," Bolan said.

"N-not yet," Norwood said painfully. "Let me rest for a moment."

Bolan nodded, trying to hurry the scientist's story. "The people you met here, were they Sonnojoi?"

Norwood looked surprised. "Yes," he said. "The symposium was just a front. I was flattered by these people, and I gave a great many lectures about nuclear power and nuclear armaments. Then one day they showed up with stolen plutonium and ordered me to make them bombs—"

"Bombs!" Bolan said. "Nuclear bombs?"

"Hydrogen bombs, to be exact," Norwood replied. "When I refused, they kidnapped me and took me to a laboratory." The man looked sadly at the ground. "I—I'm not a very strong person, I'm afraid. They beat me and deprived me of food and water. Eventually I made their bombs for them. The conditions were hardly clinical. I became contaminated. When my own safety no longer factored in my feelings, I then began to worry about what kind of monsters I had unleashed with my own hands. I began to wonder exactly what they intended to do with those bombs." He coughed again.

"We must get you to a hospital," Bolan said. "Let's get out of here. I'll help you."

Norwood waved him off. "It's too late for that," he said. "Look." He rolled up his left sleeve to show Bolan several black splotches, like bruises, on his skin. "Broken blood vessels, Mr. Reeves. I'm a dead man, a fool."

"Don't be too hard on yourself," Bolan said. "Almost anyone would have done the same thing, given the circumstances."

"Would you have?"

Bolan stared at him. "How did you escape?" he asked after a moment, his attention shifting once again to the men circling the house. He looked around. They were out in the open but quite a distance from the house. If they were to move, they'd be spotted. Bolan decided that it was best to just try to wait it out. But how had they found him?

"My assistant, Mr. Maruki, snuck me out in a laundry cart and then into the trunk of his car. It was him who brought me here, to Jukai." He made a sweeping motion with his arm toward the dense forest.

"Jukai?" Bolan asked.

"Sea of Trees," Norwood said. "The forest is impenetrable. People from all over come here to commit suicide by losing themselves in it. I will do this when my time comes."

"Where was the laboratory where they forced you to build the bombs?"

"I'm not sure. I was either blindfolded or in a car trunk. The Sonnojoi had a name for it, though. They called it *chikatetsu*."

That word again, the same one Prine had used in La Bomba before he died. "I'm going to need names," Bolan said, watching down the hill. Several figures had left the house and were moving slowly up the hill toward them. "Damn. We're going to have to—"

The Executioner's last words were swallowed in the huge explosion that turned Norwood's house into a black-and-orange ball of destruction that billowed into the crisp air, leaving behind a small fire storm and screaming neighborhood children.

Bolan was up, helping Norwood to his feet. "The forest!" he yelled. "Make for the forest!"

They were moving up the slope toward him now, eight, no ten of them, dressed in black and still wearing their black helmets. Before they had been moving dots against a placid landscape. Now they were the enemy—targets.

Norwood ran toward the woods as Bolan pulled Big Thunder and took long aim at one of them. He squeezed one off, and it kicked mud at the man's feet. The Executioner adjusted, sighting higher, and took the man out, dead center, his body tumbling backward and rolling down the slope.

The men charged him, blasting with their shotguns as they came. Ground churned near him, but the Sonnojoi were definitely at a disadvantage—running uphill and trying to fire at the same time. Bolan crouched and picked another target, a man who had stopped to aim. He hit him in the head, and the man spun around on one foot in a comical dance, then fell straight backward.

They kept coming, only a few meters separated them. Bolan kicked the legs out from under another. The man fell forward and slid downhill in the slick mud.

"Reeves!" Norwood called, and Bolan turned toward the sound.

A black unmarked helicopter, which looked like a surplus Huey, set down near the forest, blocking Norwood. Several Sonnojoi had jumped from the machine and were charging Norwood. Bolan swung Big Thunder in that direction, but he couldn't get a clear shot.

He turned back, blowing out the two men farthest up the hill, then jumped to his feet and ran toward Norwood.

Too late.

The Sonnojoi had grabbed the scientist and were running him back to the chopper. Bolan turned on the heat, running as fast as he could to close the gap between them.

They lifted Dr. Norwood into the open bay. Bolan emptied the clip into the rotors in an effort to disable the chopper, but it didn't work. As the Sonnojoi began returning fire from the open door, the squat bird rose into the morning sky. The Executioner holstered his now silent weapon and ran a serpentine course toward the bird as .12-gauge shells kicked the hell out of the ground around him.

He reached the chopper as it was still hovering just above his head. In desperation he leaped for the air-craft, grabbing one of the skids and holding on for all he was worth. The ship floundered with the uneven weight as the pilot tried to adjust. The Sonnojoi on the ground were catching up and began shooting at the man who dangled from the underside of the Huey.

Bolan locked an arm on the skid and drew his Ber-etta, returning fire, sending his pursuers ducking for cover. Men began leaning out of the bay and firing down at him, forcing him back and keeping him from swinging up onto the skid.

He looked down. They were already at tree level and still on the rise. Bolan knew that his left arm wanted to stiffen up on the skids. His hand was still weak and bleeding from the stitches of two days before. This wasn't going to work. They were nearly fifteen meters off the ground. If he was going to get down, he'd have to do it quickly or . . .

The chopper veered sharply, heading toward the forest. They had made his decision for him. They were going to try to scrape him off.

So be it.

He holstered the Beretta, grabbing the skid with both hands. A tall pine was coming at him quickly, but its height meant its branches were too thin to do him any good. He hoisted himself at the last second, and the tip of the tree just scraped him as they passed it.

He looked down at the mammoth expanse of forest, a veritable ocean of green and brown stretching thickly as far as he could see. He frantically searched the underside of the helicopter for any markings. Everything had been erased except for a small set of Japanese characters stenciled on the skid he was holding. He did his best to commit them to memory.

They were coming up on a stand of thick firs, and Bolan had to make his decision. As the Sonnojoi dipped the helicopter to try to lose him, he let go, dropping into that green sea.

He fell, crashing through the first several layers of high, thin branches. The splintering wood tore at his clothes and skin. He grabbed instinctively, just as a baby would. His hands locked and then lost hold of a thick branch.

He crashed through another, pain searing the ribs he'd hurt in the shoot-out in Junko's car, and his mind screamed that he should give up, that he should give over to the seductive darkness and let somebody else worry about it all. But Bolan's instincts were stronger, and as he blasted through a thick, dry branch with a loud crack, he was able to get his right hand out and grab hold of the stub of the limb.

His falling weight swung inward, and he hit the trunk hard, nearly losing his grip. But he held on and was able to wrap his arms around the trunk.

Bolan stayed put for a minute, taking stock, twelve meters off the ground. His body was sore, and some of his cuts had reopened, but as he systematically checked each limb and muscle, he realized that nothing was numb or broken.

Then he heard voices. The ones on the ground were coming for him. He hadn't gone deeply enough into the trees. From the sound of it, they weren't far off. He thought of staying put, simply hiding in the tree, but one look at the ground convinced him otherwise. A good-sized pile of branches and a large limb lay at the bottom of the fir. They had been knocked loose when he fell and would draw the enemy like a beacon.

He climbed quickly down the tree, jumping from limb to limb the way he had done when he was a kid. The Executioner reached the ground in a crouch, the Beretta in his hand as he scanned the terrain for targets.

The forest was not a good place for a firefight. There was too much cover for the opposition. Trees were jammed together so tightly that nothing grew at ground level, and sunshine was only able to penetrate in small dazzling sabers. Because of the density he couldn't see more than three meters from his position at any given time. It was not the place to make a stand.

He reached into his jump suit and pulled out a new clip, using his thumb to flick a bullet into his hand. Discretion at this time was by far the better part of valor. He turned from the sounds of their approach and ran deeper into the forest, dropping a bullet on the ground to mark his return path. Thirty feet later he did the same. They wouldn't be able to chase him too far;

the authorities would show up soon. When the punks turned back, he wanted to be able to do the same.

THE EXECUTIONER LET the receiver rest on his hunched-up shoulder, using his free hand to replace the bullets in the spring clip.

"That's right, Sergeant. I'm holding for Lieutenant Ichiro and I don't have much time," Bolan said.

The voice on the other end sounded far away and spoke very poor English. "Lieutenant Ichiro in very important meeting, sir. He can no come to the phone."

"Tell him Mack Bolan's on the line. And tell him to hurry."

"Meeting very important—" the man began.

"You just tell him," Bolan said. "He'll come."

The phone booth was located at the end of the covered train platform at the Fujiyoshida Station. Bolan could look out across the sloping ground and see the smoking ruins of Norwood's house on the mountainside. The black smoke was still billowing into the morning sky, spoiling the view. A number of police cars were parked around the house's charred skeleton.

Bolan looked at his watch. He was going to have to hump it to get back in time to see Hashi-san's operation in action. It was already afternoon, and it was a two-hour ride back to Shinjuku and another thirty minutes back to Yokota.

"Bolan?" came Ichiro's voice on the other end.

"Miss me?" Bolan asked. He finished reloading the clip, then jammed it into the butt of the AutoMag and holstered the weapon.

"Where are you?"

"Never mind that," Bolan replied. "There was an explosion out by Lake Yamanaka today. You need to pull your people away from it and get experts in nuke technology out there with their instruments. There's a high level of radiation at the site."

"How do you know that?"

"I was there. You're wasting time."

There was a pause on the line as Ichiro considered his options, finally settling on his gut feelings about Bolan. "Will you hold while I make the call?" he asked.

"If you promise not to try and trace this line."

"You have my word."

"Fair enough."

Bolan was put on hold, and he listened to a musical version of "Sukiyaki," which seemed to be the national song of tourist Japan, playing in the background. Within two minutes he could see the police cars pulling back from the scene of the fire and driving to the other houses to evacuate them. Once again Bolan found himself impressed with Ichiro.

The lieutenant came back on the line. "What's it all about, Bolan?" he asked.

Bolan quickly filled in as much detail on what had happened as he could without interfering with any of his other plans.

"You could have told me this the other night," Ichiro said when Bolan was finished.

"But I didn't," Bolan replied.

"We have been searching for Dr. Norwood for a long time."

"The Sonnojoi have him. Do you have a line on their meeting places?"

"Unfortunately, no," Ichiro replied. "We haven't been able to crack them yet."

"It makes no sense. A group like that would have to go public eventually. How would they gain converts?"

"It's a mystery," Ichiro said. "And I have a question for you. How did the Sonnojoi know to come to Yamanaka today, the day that you go there?"

"I don't know," Bolan replied. "I'm worried about that."

"You seem to at least have enough sense to worry," Ichiro said in exasperation. "Come in, Bolan. Give yourself up. Together we may be able to solve this thing."

"From behind bars?" Bolan said. "No, thanks."

"Without you we have nothing. No doctor, no mysterious helicopter...the Sonnojoi even took the bodies of their dead with them. I'm going to get you one way or the other, anyway. Come in now and share the information."

A train whistle blew, and Bolan used his hand to cover the mouthpiece so that Ichiro wouldn't get any ideas. His train was being announced. He'd have to go.

"I'll give you a word," Bolan said. "I think it's a key to these bastards. *Chikatetsu.*"

"What? Bolan, I—"

The Executioner hung up the phone and ran to catch his train. On the platform he watched the crowd of Japanese faces all around him. Was one of them there to watch him, to follow him? Ichiro had all but said it on the phone, the same thing that had been bothering him. Perhaps Bolan himself had been responsible, through negligence, for what had happened to Dr. Norwood. The thought nagged him all the way back to Yokota.

8

Bolan walked down the line of Japanese in their khaki uniforms. They stood at attention, M-16s strapped to their backs, extra ammo dangling from their bandoliers. They wore black berets. Just like the Seals, the Executioner thought, then realized that he was going into a Nam-like conflict, only this time the jungle was all sharp edges and etched in concrete.

"Who trained them?" Bolan asked Dr. Mett, who strode beside him, dressed in the same uniform.

"I did," Mett said proudly. "They've all been through my equivalent of your boot camp and have distinguished themselves at one time or another."

"You've done this before?"

"Several times," Mett said. "But this is the biggest operation we've undertaken yet."

"Where did you pick up your knowledge?"

"I was a merc in Korea, Nam, El Salvador, Costa Rica, Nicaragua...."

"A businessman, eh?" Bolan replied.

"I've always believed in a cause, Mr. Bolan."

"As long as the money was right."

"Everybody has to make a living. I have a doctorate in philosophy but the pay that goes along with it isn't so good."

They reached the end of the line. Junko stood there, dressed as the others. Bolan had begun to take her dual responsibilities for granted. He looked into her eyes and was met with the same blind intensity he'd seen from her in combat situations.

It was chilling and in many ways exciting.

Bolan turned and strode back to stand at the center of the formation. His black nightclothes and combat harness stood out in stark contrast to the uniforms of Hashi-san's men, the security force of Asano Corporation. Only in Japan could a man command the power and loyalty of his employees to such an extent. Only in Japan could a private army such as Hashi-san's be allowed to exist at all. The old man had declared that business ran the government. Tonight Mack Bolan was going to see that theory in action.

They were standing in an Asano warehouse somewhere between the Yokota and Tachikowa Air Bases. The building was old and badly in need of repair; the ubiquitous rain leaked through the roof in a hundred different places. It was empty save for the security force and their vehicles and several portable floodlights that illuminated the damp interior. Just outside the perimeter of light sat Hashi-san himself, dressed in traditional robes. Occasionally he nodded his head.

Bolan looked the group up and down and then spoke. The mercenary translated into Japanese. "Dr

Mett assures me that you have been well trained and well briefed for this operation. We're going to hit a cocaine factory that fronts as a coffee company. If our suspicions are correct, this operation will be worth many millions of dollars to its operators and so will be heavily defended. Our intelligence indicates that the cocaine operation takes place once a week and that civilian employees of the coffee company will not be working.

"I am in charge tonight. Our plan will only succeed if you follow your orders. You all know your specific tasks. I urge you to perform them quickly and without delay. I want the entire operation to last no more than fifteen minutes, and even at that we'll be cutting it close with the local authorities. Good luck."

White Mett prepared the vans for departure, Bolan walked over to where Hashi-san sat. The man was staring at him intently. "You will kill many Sonnojoi tonight and destroy this white poison for me," the old man said.

"No, not only for you," Bolan replied. "For everyone. It's the right thing to do."

"You are a man of great principles."

"Or great foolishness."

"No!" Hashi-san said loudly and stamped his foot. "Honor is not foolishness. The code of Bushido is not foolishness. You and I, we are the glue that holds civilization together. There is nothing foolish about that."

Bolan bowed low. "My apologies, Hashi-san."

The man smiled widely. "I like you to call me that. I like many things about you."

"And I you."

Hashimoto's face became serious. "When this is over, I could make Japan a safe place for someone with a past. You could stop running, Bolan. Our small island is a beautiful and varied country. A man could spend a lifetime here."

"Let's live through tonight first," the Executioner said as he heard Mett call him. "The trucks are ready. I must go. I'll try and keep an eye on Junko."

"She will take care of herself," Hashimoto said without inflection. "Just see that you destroy the white powder."

Bolan nodded and walked toward the vans. There were four of them, all fitted out like local produce delivery trucks. Bolan's force of twenty divided themselves into the vans, and the four vehicles rumbled out of the warehouse.

Junko drove one of the vans, and Bolan sat in the passenger's seat. He'd seen her driving before and trusted her implicitly. They shared a smile as she changed gears to follow the others onto the gravel road.

"Nervous?" he asked.

"Yes," she returned. "You?"

He took a long breath. "I don't know if it's nerves. Something stinks, and I don't know what it is. But I do know I'm tired of being led around by the nose."

"Tonight should clarify feelings." Junko turned off the gravel service road onto the Oume-Kaido Road in the direction of downtown Tokyo. "We've planned this operation for a long time. It will be a big one."

"How did you get on to it?" he asked.

"We had some contact with minor Yakuza, Japanese mafia. They're secretive, but nothing like Sonnojoi. Through bribes and threats we found that the coca bushes come from six thousand feet up in the Andes, along with the coffee beans. Yakuza-controlled companies do all the shipping and delivery. A warehouse foreman at the coffee company separates the real beans from the coca bushes. Once a week the shipments come in. Once a week, on Wednesdays, they process. We've been watching the pickups and deliveries for months."

"Have you ever seen American military personnel pick up cocaine?"

"All the time. Do you think that this is your Operation Snowflake?"

"Yeah." He turned and stared at her in the lights of passing autos. The shadows highlighted her fragile beauty. Bolan was usually so good at turning everything off save the job at hand, usually so good at pretending he wasn't human, but Junko kept breaking through the facade, getting to him. He fought down a rush of feelings. "What does the word *chikatetsu* mean to you?" he asked.

She looked at him for just a second before returning her gaze to the road. She shrugged. "Underground. Subway. That's what the dark man said at the gambling club last night.''

"Right before he died."

She nodded. *"Hai,"* she said softly. "I prayed to his ancestors this morning."

"Does that make any sense to you? Could the subway be a hiding place for the Sonnojoi?"

Again she shrugged. "I don't know. I suppose it's possible, although it seems there would be very few entry points that wouldn't be public."

Bolan sank against the back of the seat. "That's what I thought."

The talk tapered off as they sped into the city proper and turned down Aoyama-Dori, moving toward the harbor. They were psyching themselves up, mentally preparing to face the enemy, to perhaps face their own ends. The only other time Junko spoke was when they passed Tokyo Tower.

"My father built the tower," she said proudly. It resembled the Eiffel Tower, but at three hundred and thirty-three meters, it was one of the largest free-standing steel structures in the world.

Bolan could smell the harbor before he could see it, that unmistakable odor of sweet decay that accompanied nonflowing shallows. The buildings became less fancy and more utilitarian, large rusted tin structures. And then Tokyo Harbor stretched before them, a small spot of calm in the raging infinity of the Pacific Ocean. Large freighters filled the dock spaces, loading and unloading going on even at night.

"Look," Junko said, pointing.

Through the swishing wipers Bolan could see it, a large, two-story tin building several docks away. Tanazaki Kohi Ltd. was written under a huge painting of a steaming cup of coffee.

"Binoculars are under the seat," Junko said, and Bolan took out the large unit, switching on the infrared attachment as he put it to his face.

This was the place, all right. The building terraced like a wedding cake. Bolan could make out a number of Sonnojoi armed with what appeared to be scopes attached to their Ruger Mini-14s. From their positions the guards commanded a panoramic view of the terrain in all directions.

The vans slid behind the cover of a rotting dock two hundred meters from the building. The Asano people climbed out of the vehicles and silently handed their equipment around.

Bolan walked up to Mett, who was helping unload a crate of C-4 plastique. "We're going to have to deal with those lookouts," he said.

Mett smiled and walked to the back of his van, pulling out a rifle wrapped in a blanket. He handed it to Bolan.

The Executioner pulled the blanket off a Weatherby Mark V, .460 Magnum, a hunting rifle of righteous proportions. The scope, like the binoculars, was infrared.

"Seen one before?" Mett asked.

"Yeah," Bolan said, thinking of a day in Tehran several years before. He stared at the bolt-action, single-shot weapon. "There's seven of them up there on that building and you people have a lot of ground to cover to get there."

Mett handed him a box of shells. "It was Hashisan's idea," he said.

Bolan looked at the man and began to realize exactly how seriously they all took the Bushido code. He turned to the others, who were standing silently around him, waiting.

"Ask them," Bolan told Mett.

The doctor shrugged and spoke to the group in Japanese, everyone responding with smiles and nods of encouragement. They were all of them, to a man, betting their lives on the Executioner's ability as a marksman.

Bolan took a deep breath. "Okay," he said, "I'll play."

Just then they heard trucks rumbling down onto the dock area. They pulled back into the shadows and watched as a small Air Force convoy moved past their position. Two covered deuce-and-a-halfs and two covered jeeps roared by, grinding toward the coffee company.

Bolan moved to peer around the edge of the dock to see a shadowy figure waving from atop the building. Junko was at his elbow.

"Your Operation Snowflake?" she asked.

"Yeah," Bolan said. "Maybe." He turned to Mett. "There's no other approach to that place?"

Mett shook his head. "It's located on a point of land. This is the only approach where we could conceivably get away when it is over."

Bolan looked at the building again. The convoy had gone around the building, disappearing from view. "Have your men ready," he told Mett. "Spread them out and keep to the shadows. When I say the word, go for it. We'll regroup at the building and all go in together. Junko, you stay with me. We'll use the van when I'm finished."

Bolan handed Junko the rifle and shells, then moved to one of the parked vans. Jumping, he got a grip on the top rails and hauled himself onto the roof of the vehicle. Junko handed him the hardware from the ground. Bolan could easily reach the wharf roof from the top of the van. He placed his weapon on the roof of the building, then climbed up moving across the cracking boards until he reached the peak of the roof. From here he had an unobstructed view of the complex.

He flexed his fingers, loosening them, and then squatted in a comfortable position. On the range years ago he had tested the Mark V. The best time he had been capable of achieving was about six seconds to load, aim, fire, bolt and reload. That meant forty-two seconds to kill seven men—providing he didn't miss. He assumed that, as soon as his force was spotted, those inside would be alerted. It would take about a minute for his men to reach the tin building, not enough time for those within to be truly prepared. It could work *if* his aim was perfect. If it wasn't, the men on the roof would kick hell out of his squad with their Rugers and they'd be lost before they started.

It was a dangerous game with his men as the bait to keep the Sonnojoi on their feet and shooting. Otherwise, it would be a standoff—the enemy would hide and wait.

"Ready," he whispered loudly and in response heard his men run toward their positions. Bolan lined up seven of the big shells on the flat peak, then pulled back the bolt and slid one of them into the chamber. He closed the bolt and took a deep breath. The rifle would make plenty of noise. No one would doubt what was going on. This was a game of time—of seconds—they were playing. And it was all Hashi-san's idea. The man had an intricate, multilayered mind.

The Executioner breathed again, isolating himself from everything extraneous to the task ahead. He emptied his mind of all thought except the mechanics of loading, firing and hitting the target. It was a metaphysical thing, very Zen, very Japanese.

He raised the rifle, resting the recoil pad snugly against his shoulder. Mind now clear, Bolan flicked on the scope and sighted through the wavering red cross hairs. He would be methodical. The building tiered in three layers, with one man at the top. He would take the top man first, then move left to right down each tier, taking out each man as he sighted in on him.

The cross hairs found the first man easily. He was moving around nervously. The punk was jumpy. Bolan thumbed off the safety and led his target slightly. He breathed again, totally calm, an island of tranquility. This was it.

"Go," he rasped, and at the same instant squeezed the trigger. The first man spun under the impact of a chest hit, and Bolan snapped back the bolt before he even saw the man fall.

The shell sprang from the chamber, along with a whiff of smoke, and the Executioner shoved another shell in to replace it. He jammed the bolt into place and sighted on the second man. The enemy gunman was searching for the source of the gunshot. Bolan got the enemy's head in the cross hairs and squeezed off. The man's head popped, and his body tumbled forward off the building.

The next shell flew from the chamber, rattling down on the roof as Bolan reloaded in a single fluid motion. He saw the third man on a walkie-talkie, obviously alerting those inside. The Executioner ended the transmission with one shot. The radio exploded along with the punk's face.

Less than twenty seconds had gone by. The fourth man had spotted the charging Asanos and was sighting with his Ruger. Bolan fired chest high, thinking for a second that he'd missed the man when he continued to stand, holding his rifle. Then the Sonnojoi folded quietly, crumpling to the rooftop as his rifle plunged off the building.

Damn! Bolan had lost several seconds watching the last hit. He hurried through the reloading process, taking a second to calm himself again before sighting the fifth man.

Before he found the man, the sound of gunfire assailed the Executioner's ears. His squad was now under enemy fire from a superior position. Bolan swung to the fifth man, who was firing rapidly. He hurried the shot, only taking the fleshy part of the man's shoulder, but it was enough to make him drop his rifle over the edge.

He fought down anger at himself and reloaded, taking a breath as he sighted the sixth man and squeezed him off cleanly with a chest hit. Only one rifle was now firing at his men. Less than forty seconds had elapsed.

Bolan bolted, then reached for the last shell. His hand hit it, knocking it off the small ledge to rattle down the roof. His instincts kicked in, and his hand flashed down to catch the shell in midbounce. He chambered it, swung the rifle to the seventh man and fired. An animal sound escaped his lips as the gunner's head exploded on the other end.

The rifle was of no more use to him. Bolan dropped it, then ran down the sloping roof and jumped onto the top of the van. "Go!" he screamed to Junko, who jerked into gear immediately and roared off. Bolan grabbed the top handrail and held on with one hand while drawing Big Thunder from his hip holster with the other.

They sped along the docks and past numerous storage buildings before catching up to and then passing the now charging squad. Junko braked, and the van skidded to a stop directly below the painting of the coffee cup. Bolan jumped from the roof and ran to a door at the base of the structure. His men were running up as he tested it. Locked.

It was a metal door set in metal. Mett pushed his way to the door and pulled out a hand grenade.

"Back off!" Bolan yelled as Mett pulled the pin, balancing the grenade on the doorknob. They all took cover just as the explosion echoed across the sounding board of Tokyo Harbor.

Bolan's group moved back to the blackened, gutted hole that had once been a door. The Executioner primed Big Thunder, its stainless steel glinting under the lights from inside. He was charged for this, in control at last. "You know what to do!" he yelled and ran into the guts of the building, his men right behind.

They were in the building's plumbing, a maze of various sizes of water, steam and natural-gas pipes that crisscrossed above their heads and on ground level.

"C-4 here!" he yelled. "Set the timer for twelve minutes!"

As a demolition man hurried to comply, Bolan kept running. There was no time now for stealth or caution. He knew that it had to be straight-out guts baseball.

They charged through the concrete room toward a series of small steps at the far end. Four Sonnojoi were charging down the stairs with their Remingtons. Bolan's men were ready, and soon the basement rattled with the trill of fifteen M-16s.

The blasts literally cut the Sonnojoi to ribbons, and body parts and organs splattered against the chipping concrete walls.

Bolan's group charged up the blood-spattered stairs toward a door that led to a locker room. A handful of Sonnojoi had taken up positions there and were able to concentrate fire on the doorway, holding Bolan's people back. The smell of gunpowder mixed with the strong odor of freshly roasted coffee.

"Grenades!" the Executioner called, and Mett was there again, his face, as always, calm and placid.

He had a pouchful of grenades and began lobbing them, one after another, into the locker room, mixing his directions and velocity. After several seconds they began exploding, and the thin metal lockers that lined the room became deadly, ripping shrapnel. Mett continued to toss the grenades, turning the inside of the room into a rumbling, smoke-filled nightmare.

"Go!" he said finally, and Bolan was the first into the blinding smoke. He could hear a gunner still firing, but the smoke was impossible to sight through. The room was a gutted shambles of collapsed lockers and ceiling. They moved through the maze as the smoke began to clear.

The remaining gunman was hiding behind what was left of a round cement urinal, no more than fifteen feet away. He was pivoting toward Bolan as the big man raised the AutoMag and fired. The man pitched crazily to the left, hitting his head on the urinal.

The Asanos hurried through what was left of the room, stepping across several bodies buried in the rubble. They hit the exit arch, hugging the wall on each side before running through. Mett was on one side of the doorway, Bolan on the other, Junko at Bolan's elbow. Bolan looked at Mett, and the man shrugged in return. Bolan turned and grabbed Junko's beret off her head and threw it through the doorway. Nothing. He looked at his watch. They'd already lost a couple of minutes. There wasn't time to think about it.

Bolan ran through the doorway, tumbling and rolling. He came up in a short, dark hallway but could see the main working area of the factory beyond a glass wall and doorway. He saw no sign of resistance.

"Let's go!" he called, and they were out of the locker room and running down the hallway with Bolan and Junko in the lead.

Just as they reached the end door, three men jumped up from behind some machinery on the factory side, blasting away with their Remingtons.

Bolan ate pavement, and Junko screamed from beside him as his men fell. They were trapped in the hall under deadly fire from the shotguns. The Executioner fired from the prone position on auto, lacing one of the Sonnojoi from groin to chest. The man's insides burst through his black clothes as he fell hard.

Mett, who was behind him on one knee, claimed the next one as his M-16 dropped the man atop Bolan's kill.

The third man decided to turn and run. It was a fatal decision. Those left on their feet in the hall tore him up from behind, cutting his legs out from under him before he dropped to the floor.

Bolan turned quickly to Junko. She lay still as blood oozed from a dozen places. For a second a cold hand gripped the Executioner's heart. Then she stirred, shaking her head. A thin trickle of blood dotted her lower lip.

"I'm not dead," she said and smiled. "Only the glass hit me. Let's go."

"Wait," he said and pulled a glass shard out of her arm before helping her up. She winked at him—one tough woman.

Bolan turned. Three of his men had been wounded in the hallway, but they refused to stay behind. Bushido.

They ran into the factory and into the overpowering smell of coffee. It was a huge, open room, full of thirty-foot-tall heating vessels where green coffee beans were roasted. But this wasn't what Bolan was looking for. He wanted the machines they used to make instant coffee. The ones they'd use to process cocaine.

Bolan and his warriors came under fire immediately from catwalks located high above the brightly lit room. But they had cover and room to run. They could take these sons of bitches.

They ran serpentine-style through the room as concrete chips flew around them. "Take cover!" Bolan yelled. "Pick your targets. We don't have much time! Junko! Demolition! Follow me!"

The three of them ran into the guts of the building. Bolan had decided to leave the snipers for his men so that he could concentrate on the mission itself. They'd gone a hundred feet, past the roasters and into the maze of conveyor belts and stamping machines where the roasted and ground coffee was canned for the public, when he saw it.

The instant-coffee machine was a large, square, stainless-steel structure—an extractor—that performed several tasks. Ground coffee was filtered through water into a cooler, then dropped into a vacuum drum drier that removed the water at freezing temperature, leaving tiny, solid coffee crystals behind. Such a system worked perfectly with ground coca leaves.

The heavily guarded extractor was thirty feet away. Bolan and his party stood amid a profusion of conveyor belts that carried beans, cans and ground coffee to other parts of the building. When Bolan found the controls to turn the whole system on, the belts churned to life with a loud whine.

A belt beside them rose at a forty-five-degree angle, then straightened, moving toward the extractor. Bolan put a finger to his lips and indicated the belt. So far they hadn't been seen. He wanted to keep it that way as long as possible.

They all climbed onto the belt to take the ride up. From the diminishing fire behind them, Bolan figured his people were doing their jobs. A tribute to Mett, a man Bolan could not admire. He killed for money only, part of what was wrong with the world.

When they crested and slipped onto the horizontal conveyor, Bolan got his first look at the storage area. Hundreds of sacks with green tags were piled near the extractor. These were weighted and filled with coca leaves. Beyond that were loading docks, where uniformed military men were helping the Sonnojoi load huge bags, like feed sacks, into the backs of the trucks.

So it was all true, every bit of it. Air Force personnel were heavily involved in one of the biggest illegal drug operations Bolan had ever witnessed. It made his insides knot with rage. He'd worn the uniform proudly; all of his dedication had poured into what it represented. These men were worse than the Mafia, worse than the KGB. These men were a cancer on the reputation of the U.S. military, and they had to be destroyed at all costs.

"Time?" Junko whispered from behind him, and Bolan snapped back to the present.

He looked at his watch. "We've got less than six minutes," he said and pulled the Beretta so that he had a weapon in each hand. Death times two.

The conveyor was taking them near the extractor, three meters above it. Five nervous gunmen surrounded the machines, plus two men in white lab coats who were being forced to continue working by one of the Sonnojoi.

Bolan turned and looked at Junko. Blood oozed from several of her cuts, two on her face marring her perfect skin. She nodded and firmly locked her M-16 in her bloody hands.

"Now!" Bolan yelled, and the three of them jumped onto the top of the loudly grinding extractor.

Five shotguns turned upward, and Bolan fired down into two helmetless faces. The men hadn't stood a chance.

Two shotguns popped loudly, and Bolan's demolition man dropped his knapsackful of C-4 to clutch a gaping wound in his chest. He rolled off the machine as Junko took out his killer, her M-16 on full auto tearing off the punk's arm and opening his left side like a split melon.

The scientists ran, and Bolan let them as SMG fire rattled from the loading bays. The military was adding their firepower to that of the drug pushers.

Bolan cursed and jumped from the machine, blasting one of the Sonnojoi who was scurrying for cover. Junko got the other as he fell to his knees, begging for mercy.

Junko jumped off the machine, the knapsack looped around her arm, as the Air Force concentrated fire on her. At ground level hundreds of thousands of pounds of coffee beans separated Bolan from the Air Force. Neither could get in a shot.

The gunfire had stopped from behind, and Bolan's men were running up to join him at the extractor, which was still running and dumping conveyor loads of processed white powder onto the floor. They were surrounded by billions of dollars' worth of cocaine. Fifty-pound sacks, not yet closed, were set all around them.

Dr. Mett surveyed the scene. "Guess we did pretty damned good," he said.

Bolan grunted. "Set a charge here for three minutes," he said. "Let's gather our dead and wounded and get out the way we came in—quick!"

Everyone scattered, leaving Bolan and Junko standing by the machine. "Let's go," she said.

"Not yet," Bolan replied, snapping new clips into both his sidearms. "I've got business with the Air Force."

"There's no time...."

"Maybe. Now get out."

"No," she said simply, and he could tell by the look in her eyes that she wouldn't leave him.

They ran in the direction of the loading docks, drawing heavy fire almost immediately. Bolan gained ground by using five-foot-high stacks of bean sacks for cover, which he jumped over to the next closest aisle.

"This is taking too much time," Junko said. "We'll never make it."

Bolan silently agreed, but he jumped another aisle. The Executioner came up over a stack and fired at a Sonnojoi driving a forklift and loading a palletful of fifty-pound sacks into the back of a truck. The man slumped over the wheel and drove right off the end of the dock, crashing loudly on the concrete outside.

That was enough for the Air Force. Bolan could hear shouted orders and knew they were getting out. He abandoned his hiding place and charged out into an aisle, firing at the trucks as they pulled away from the dock.

He made the edge of the dock near a Sonnojoi who stood with his hands in the air. Bolan ignored him and kept firing at the departing trucks, although they were now too far away to stop. He emptied both clips before turning to the Sonnojoi. Junko ran up beside Bolan, and the Sonnojoi's face took on a quizzical expression as she blasted him to a meeting with his ancestors.

"We've got to get out of here!" she yelled, and Bolan nodded his agreement. They jumped off the edge of the dock and charged around the structure to find the road they had come in on.

They got around the building with mere seconds left before it blew. Mett had the dead and wounded in the van that Junko had driven up to the building and was just pulling away. The rest of the team was running behind the vehicle.

Bolan and Junko joined the flight, running like animals through a forest fire to put as much distance between themselves and the conflagration to come.

First the charge in the storage area went up with a loud whomp. There was no physical sign of the explosion until the walls and the roof began to collapse and large tongues of fire licked out of the top of the building.

"Keep running!" Bolan screamed to the stragglers, and then the basement charge went, taking out the gas lines in a devastating fireball whose concussion knocked them all to the ground.

Bolan was up first, helping Junko to her feet. The area was lit up like day from the monstrous white-hot fire that burned behind them.

"Go! Go!" They ran on, exhausted, the fire heating their backs, making them sweat. They could hear small explosions as gas motors and storage tanks blew. Cars a hundred feet from the explosions burned—the harbor area was a blazing inferno.

Sirens screamed as the group reached their vans. As they pulled away from the harbor area, they passed many fire trucks—trucks that were arriving too late to stop the hand of fate.

"WHAT'S THE CONNECTION between the coke and Dr. Norwood?" Hal Brognola asked for the third time.

Bolan leaned against the freestanding outdoor phone booth and sighed. "If I knew that, Hal, I wouldn't be asking you about it." He had unscrewed the light bulb in the booth for privacy, while Junko sat in the passenger's seat of the van, nursing her wounds. "What about those APs I asked you to find out about?"

"You've hit on something with that one," Brognola said. "All the guys you mentioned—O'Brian, Prine, Jeffries—have spent time in military jails all over the world. Prine and Jeffries were in for murder and felonious assault. Prine was also held on a rape charge. O'Brian's an even bigger fish. He was one of the key men in the NCO service club kickback scandal in 1970. He'd ripped the government off for millions before they caught him."

"How'd they get out?"

"Came up for parole and were personally vouched for by a fly-boy named Captain Jamison. He asked that they be transferred to serve under him as APs at Yokota. It's all on the up-and-up as far as the government's concerned, but I checked into Jamison's background and found out that he was a lieutenant colonel who was busted in Vietnam for atrocities."

"What sort of atrocities?"

"He enjoyed napalming villages, Mack—any kind of villages. Friend, foe, you name it. He liked to watch them burn."

"Good God. Can you do anything on your end?"

"Start an investigation," Hal Brognola said. "But that won't do us any good right now. If you only had more proof..."

"You didn't send me over here to find proof, Hal. You sent me over to ice those bastards."

Silence on the other end.

"What about Hashimoto?" he asked, looking at Junko again. She was staring at him with sad eyes.

"Clean as a whistle. He was a noncombatant in the Second World War, apparently hid out in the mountains to resist the draft. After the war he helped rebuild Japan's economy, especially the steel industry. He's done so well that he's managed to undercut American steel and keep us from competing in the world market. What does he have to do with this?"

"Not sure," Bolan said. "Anything else?"

"Yeah, Mack. Take care of yourself."

"Sure."

Bolan hung up and left the booth, moving quickly around to the driver's side of the van. He climbed in, and Junko turned her head to smile at him.

"You sure you don't need to go to a hospital?" he asked.

She shook her head. "What's your American word...super...something?"

"Superficial."

"Yes. My wounds are superficial. I want you to take care of them."

"All right." He drove back to his safehouse. Junko slept for most of the trip. When Bolan walked around the van and opened her door, she looked at him through heavy-lidded eyes.

"Hello," she said sleepily and didn't resist when he picked her up and carried her into the house.

He took her into the bedroom and set her down on his *futon*, hurrying back to the car to retrieve the first-aid kit that each van was furnished with.

He came back into the bedroom to find her fully awake. She had taken her uniform off and was sitting, naked, on the sleeping cushions. "You'll take better care of me than any doctor," she said.

He moved to her, his mouth dry. She was exquisite, a fluttering wounded bird totally dependent upon him. He opened the kit and took out bandages and antiseptic.

"You should bathe first," he said.

She lowered her head and looked up at him.

Bolan wanted this woman badly. She understood him and the underlying sense of duty that drove him. She was a small voice crying out to him that he wasn't totally inhuman, that his quest hadn't deadened him completely. And most of all, he saw the same things in her and knew that her need was just as strong.

And when they made love it was slow, with understanding and genuine caring, both of them reaching out for what was caring in the other and cherishing it until they both cried out in their passion and mutual need.

And then Mack Bolan slept. He slept so deeply that he didn't hear her crying softly in the night.

9

The deck overlooked Lake Ashi from a height of several hundred feet. Bolan leaned against the rail and stared out at the beautiful placidity of Ashi, nestled in an emerald-green bowl of forests and volcanic mountains. In the distance a cable car moved silently toward the sulphurous peak of Mount Kamiyama. Hashi-san stood silently beside him, hands behind his back, contemplating the serenity that stretched around them.

"Life can be filled with so many wondrous experiences," Bolan said softly.

"And so many hideous ones," Hashi-san replied, completing the Executioner's thought. "The great dichotomy. A man like you sees both sides. You have become an instrument of karma, you know. You help maintain the balance of the two extremes."

"I wish I believed that." Bolan turned away from the lake to stare at Hashi-san's magnificent palatial home nestled in the foothills of Mount Kamiyama. "I fear the dark side takes more than its share, that it threatens to swallow us."

"That is why you are such a good karmic weapon," the small man returned, smiling broadly. "Dr. Mett tells me you did extremely well last night."

They had begun to walk back toward the house. Junko, wrapped in silks, her hair done up with flowers, knelt in her garden. A traditional Japanese garden, it contained several small bonsai trees, plus bamboo and wildflowers. Carefully arranged rocks and an ornamental stone lantern completed the scene. It was a place of beauty and order.

They stopped near Junko. She looked up shyly, then bent her head, blushing, and returned to her flower arranging.

"I want you to understand something," Bolan told the man. "The only reason I used your rifle was because your people expected it and I saw no other way into the building at that moment. That was a far too dangerous approach and endangered the lives of too many of my men."

Hashi-san laughed, nodding vigorously. "You are a warrior, Bolan-san, a Bushido warrior. You did it out of loyalty to your leader and out of love of the challenge."

"I told you two days ago," Bolan said. "I answer to no one but myself."

Hashimoto stopped smiling and stared hard at him. "You don't know yet who or what you serve," he said. "You have followed your heart and the heart knows no reason."

Bolan bowed slightly. "Out of respect, I accept your definition."

Hashi-san laughed again, patting Bolan on the arm. "Good, good." He gestured toward Junko. "You look upon my daughter with bright eyes."

Bolan looked at the young woman. "She's a good fighter," he said. "A good . . . friend."

"Hai," the old man said. "You think maybe my eyesight's so bad I cannot see." He pulled off his wire-rimmed glasses.

Bolan and Hashi-san shared a look, and Bolan saw something very catlike in the man's face. He took Bolan by the arm.

"Come," he said. "I tire. We'll sit down and make plans." He spoke to Junko in Japanese, and the young woman hurried to her feet and ran off without looking at either of them.

The old man began to walk, and Bolan moved with him. "Junko is a fine girl," Hashi-san said. "She will bear fine sons. She is a cultured girl, not just the fighter you have seen. She grew up in the schools of ikebana, the art you saw her practicing in the garden. She may be too educated for most men, but somehow I do not think a man like you would fear that in a woman."

Bolan stared at him. They continued to walk through the garden, its tiny diverging pathways beginning to resemble a sophisticated spiderweb. Stone stairs led up from the garden to a wide veranda, which was surrounded by a short stone wall topped by small, well-sculpted hedges. Three full glasses waited for them on a table in the middle of the veranda.

The magnificence of rural Japan rose around them as they sat. It would be easy, Bolan thought, for a man to get lost here. And he surprised himself with the thought. It wasn't one he usually entertained.

"Iced tea," Hashi-san said, picking up his tall glass. "One of the few civilized practices invented by Western society." He took a small sip, letting the tea sit in his mouth before swallowing it.

Bolan followed suit. "You have a problem with Western civilization?" he asked.

Hashi-san shook his head. "Life is change," he said. "The West gave us technology, a force in life that means change. Good, bad, who knows? The Orient invented gunpowder and used it to make fireworks. The Europeans made cannons with it. Different approaches. The secret of life today is in keeping up with change."

"I understand that you've beaten the West at its own game technologically," Bolan said.

"It's a game anyone can play," Hashi-san replied, shrugging. "What game is it that you're playing?"

"I don't understand."

The old man gestured wide. "I've opened my life to you. You know my deepest secrets yet you keep many secrets from me. Junko tells me that you have made two transoceanic phone calls. And now you're referring to my technological games with the West. If you want to know about me, why don't you ask? My respect for you grows by the minute, Mr. Bolan. There is nothing I won't tell you."

"I've lived for many years in the world of shadows, Hashi-san," Bolan replied, suppressing a feeling of guilt. "As you said, the instrument of karma. Trust is something I cannot afford if I'm to stay alive."

The large smile was back. "You are simply a *ronin* looking for a master," he said. "Place your trust in me. I can be father and protector and country to you."

Just then Junko came through the sliding-glass door from the house, bearing a silver tray piled high with rice cakes. Eyes downcast, she set the tray in the middle of the table, then stood off to the side.

"You may sit, Daughter," Hashi-san said.

"Domo arigato," she replied, taking the empty seat.

"I was just telling Bolan-san that he doesn't trust us enough," Hashi-san said.

"Each answers his own calling, Father," she replied. "Mr. Bolan does not owe—"

"Wait," Bolan said. "There's no reason at this stage for secrecy on my part. I'm sorry if I've offended you in any way, Hashi-san."

"No offense taken, my son," Hashi-san replied.

Bolan told them the story then, leaving nothing out. Hashi-san listened intently to the story of Dr. Norwood and Operation Snowflake, nodding from time to time. He seemed relieved when Bolan was finished.

"This is no great secret," the old man said. "In fact, it is a relief. My influence and channels of information run deep. Perhaps I can help you with your mission, and then we can look onward to other things.''

"Other things?'' Bolan asked.

"I say in front of my ancestors that I want you to stay with me and help me run my organization,'' Hashi-san replied, taking another small sip of iced tea. "You are a man of ideas and ideals, a man not afraid to put those feelings into action. If I help you with this problem, perhaps I can clear your mind enough that you will think about these things.''

"I'm always open to suggestions,'' Bolan answered, honored at the man's admission. Then a thought occurred to him. "I saw some Japanese characters written on the skid of the helicopter that kidnapped Dr. Norwood. If I wrote them down, could you translate them for me?''

"I will do my best,'' Hashi-san said, bowing.

Junko was sent for paper and pencil, her fingers and Bolan's stopping for a lingering touch when she handed them to him.

The big man sat down and tried to recreate the moment in his mind, closing his eyes to bring the look of the characters into sharp focus. He wrote the characters just the way he remembered them, then slid the paper over to Hashi-san.

The man looked at it for a minute, then raised his eyebrows. "Ah, your kanji could use some improvement, but I think I see what you want. Unfortunately, I think it will be of little help. You have written the characters for the bit of snow, or snowflake.''

"Why would something so secret be written on equipment?" Bolan asked. "Perhaps this is a company or something, a business with that name."

Hashi-san grunted. "I will have my people look into it for you."

"Thank you," Bolan said, then added, "Is it possible for me to borrow a car from you? I think I'm going to shake up the situation a bit."

"What's mine is yours," Hashi-san said. "I will have Dr. Mett bring something around for you."

"Would you like...someone to go with you?" Junko asked.

Bolan shook his head. "Not this time. Where I'm going no one but me can get in."

LIEUTENANT KENDO ICHIRO SAT on the shiny yellow plastic bench at Shinjuku Station and thought about all the trouble he was going to get into over this one. The travelers and shoppers were lined up near the platform, waiting for the trains that he had used emergency authorization to halt while the *chikatetsu* tunnels were searched by his men.

The station like most train stations in Japan, was buried under a shopping mall of stores and restaurants. At this moment he was staring at the bottom level of the Odakyu Department Store. Perhaps they'd need a floorwalker if he lost his job over this. He might not mind the convenience of such a job, he thought. In Tokyo it was possible to travel by train from a distance, shop all day, watch a film and eat dinner without once ever walking out into the sunshine or leaving the station. Progress.

Meanwhile, he thought about Bolan and the mark he'd left all over the city. From the pachinko parlor explosion to the highway massacre to the fight at La Bomba to the destruction of the plant on the docks, he saw the indelible fingerprints of the Executioner. The man was doing Ichiro's job for him in ways that the lieutenant knew he never could. Unfortunately, the entire country was in an uproar. So, while he checked out leads suggested by Bolan, his superiors were screaming for the same man's head. The investigation of the subway system was a desperate attempt to justify Bolan's actions. If it failed to uncover anything, he'd have to go after the big man with everything he had, perhaps at the expense of losing to the Sonno-joi.

The walkie-talkie sitting beside him squawked loudly. He picked it up, dreading the worst. "Ichiro," he said.

"This is Natsume," came the static reply.

"What do you have?"

"We've found three drunks and hundreds of wild cats and dogs," Ichiro's assistant said. "After that, all we've come across is some substandard tunnel repair."

Ichiro sighed loudly. "Make a note of the areas that need work, then bring everybody back. We'll need to get these trains running as quickly as possible."

Ichiro turned the walkie-talkie off and rose slowly from the bench. When they got through with him, he'd be lucky to have an ass to sit on. He shouldn't have listened to Bolan, but there was something, something about *chikatetsu* that rang a bell with him. He just couldn't quite place it.

BOLAN PULLED THE MERCEDES sports car across the street from the main gate of Yokota Air Base to a spot in front of the Boston Tailor shop. His weapons were locked securely in the trunk. The owner of the shop told Bolan that he was an ex-lifer who had fallen in love with the country he'd been stationed in and had decided to stay when his tour was over. He was more than happy with the twenty dollars Bolan offered him to watch the car.

Bolan waited out the thick traffic, then ran across the wide boulevard to come up near the gate.

It was time, he'd decided, to make a move. He'd kicked them in the ass hard enough to scare them, probably into picking up stakes and moving on. Now that he had the quarry running, it was time to flush it out into the open. It was a dangerous game he was playing, but one that was necessary. He'd heard enough from Hal Brognola on the phone to know that any real action was going to have to come from his end. Bolan knew that government wheels grind too slowly to catch the quick red fox. It was up to him. Always. And from the look of how much coke the Air Force had hauled away from the docks, the outcome would be of deadly importance to a great many people.

Bolan walked through the gate and past the AP shack sitting beside it. A tech sergeant walked out of the shack to intercept him. He didn't recognize this one, but he bet there were people in the hut who recognized *him*.

"Halt!" the sergeant said, and Bolan accommodated him.

"Hello," Bolan said casually, pulling his Charles Reeves passport out of his back pocket, and handing it to the man. "No rain for once."

"No, sir," the sergeant returned in clipped tones. He looked at the passport. "What business do you have here, Mr. Reeves?"

"I'm an American citizen visiting American soil," Bolan replied. "Do I need more of a reason than that?"

"There have been problems lately," the AP began, "with terrorists."

"You have the right to search me for weapons, Sergeant," Bolan said. "But beyond that, this is the U.S. taxpayers' property and I'm a taxpayer. You can't keep me out."

"Will you step against the wall, sir?" the man requested politely and then searched Bolan when he complied.

"All right," the AP said, his disappointment obvious. "You can go in. You have access to all parts of the base except the flight line, which is restricted to everyone without proper authorization.''

"I understand," Bolan said and walked into the base.

It was a huge base, one of the largest in the world. It had served the Japanese Air Force well during the Second World War and was performing a similar function for America now. Should Japan be successful in dislodging the U.S. from its soil, it would undoubtedly house the Japanese Air Force again.

He walked north, past the BX, toward a cluster of white frame buildings that undoubtedly made up Base Ops. Bolan knew that General Wentworth was the CO. He was the man the Executioner intended to talk things over with.

Bolan found the building that housed the general by asking around, then simply walked across the small, manicured lawn, up the wooden stairs and into the reception area.

A Waf in an E-3's uniform sat behind a desk, pounding away on an old manual typewriter. She looked up in surprise when he walked in, not expecting to see anyone wearing civilian clothes on the base.

"Hi," Bolan said.

"Can I help you?"

"The general in there?" He pointed to a door that had Base Commander on it.

"Yes, but..."

"Don't get up." Bolan smiled. "I'll surprise him."

He hurried to the door before she could intercept him and walked right in. The general looked up in astonishment when he entered.

"What do you want?" the gray-haired man demanded.

"Five minutes of your time," Bolan said.

The woman came in right behind Bolan. "General Wentworth, I'm sorry, but—"

"I'm here to save you from being drummed out of the service in disgrace, sir," Bolan said. "Believe me, five minutes, no more."

Everything stopped. Wentworth picked a green cigar out of a beanbag ashtray and lit it, puffing vigorously. "Wait outside, Davis," he told the clerk. "If this man isn't out of here in five minutes, call the Air Police."

"Yes, sir!" the woman said and disappeared.

"This better be good, Mr...."

"Reeves," Bolan said and leaned against the desk. "I'll make it very simple. You have a captain in your command named Jamison. I assume he's CO in charge of the Air Police...."

Wentworth puffed on his cigar without saying anything, so Bolan continued.

"Captain Jamison is a renegade, busted down from colonel during the Vietnam War. He's gone to a great deal of trouble to fill his command with ex-convicts, people he's carefully pulled from parole hearings all over the world. I strongly suspect that Captain Jamison and his men have been engaged in a large-scale operation code-named Operation Snowflake that is flying tons of pure cocaine to American air bases. Their activities also include murder, and they are involved in the disappearance of a top American scientist.''

"Do you have any proof of these preposterous allegations?'' the general asked casually, though Bolan could tell that the calm was forced.

"I personally watched an Air Force convoy last night pick up a shipment of cocaine from a factory on Tokyo Harbor that processed it. The factory has been destroyed. You might have seen it in the papers.''

The general remained silent.

"I also was involved in a firefight with several of your APs in Tokyo the night before. They were in the process of trading cocaine for the bodies of innocent Japanese girls. I know you've heard about that one.''

Wentworth nodded. "Why do you come to me now?''

"They've got to be stopped, and soon. I can't do it alone. You, as base commander, have power over this installation. You can search it, you can stop anything.''

"*If* I believe you,'' Wentworth said and looked at his watch. "Your time is almost up.''

"*Don't* believe me,'' Bolan said. "Check the records on your APs. See where they're all coming from and ask yourself why.''

Wentworth took the cigar out of his mouth and wrote something on a piece of paper. He handed it to

Bolan. "This is a direct line in here," he said. "Call me in a few hours."

"You won't regret this," Bolan said.

He left the office just as the clerk was picking up her phone to call the APs.

"There's no need," he said. "They already know I'm here."

He left and walked right back to the main gate, waving to the tech sergeant who'd frisked him coming in. He crossed the street, fiddling around in the car long enough to make sure they wouldn't lose him, then pulled away when he saw the jeep sliding up to the gate.

"GOOD GOD," General Wentworth said as he stood staring at the printout Rebecca Davis had handed him. "Have you looked at this?"

The clerk nodded solemnly.

Wentworth looked at the list again. "This whole outfit should be on death row," he said. "And all of them personally vouched for and recommended by Jamison."

"Perhaps he just believes in giving men a second chance," Davis offered.

"Not *these* men," Wentworth said angrily. "Not on my base. I'm going to shove this printout in that bastard's face. I'll be right back. Meanwhile, get the Pentagon on the line."

Wentworth clumsily folded the printout and stuck it in his back pocket. He strode purposefully out the door, slamming it behind him. Rebecca Davis stared at the door for a moment, then picked up the phone.

Her call did not go through to the Pentagon.

CAPTAIN HANK JAMISON LISTENED attentively to the woman on the phone, trying to speak to her in as calm a voice as he could muster.

"Becky," he said softly. "Take it easy. This is no big deal. It's just a misunderstanding. I'll clear it up as soon as the General gets here. Meanwhile, you sit tight.... No, don't call Washington. It'll just embarrass the general. We'll all have a laugh about this later. Okay. I love you, too. Yeah ... Bye."

His hands clenched the desk in rage, his knuckles white. "That son of a bitch," he said hoarsely. "That damned son of a bitch."

His insides were on fire. He looked at his watch. They were a day away from completing this operation, and there was no way that Wentworth or that damned civilian were going to slow him down. He'd just have to do what it took.

There was an angry knock on his office door, and then General Wentworth barged in.

"After all I've done for you, Hank," the man said, red-faced. "After all I've done for you."

"What's wrong?" Jamison asked calmly.

The general pulled a printout from his back pocket and held it in a shaking fist. "I stood up for you when nobody else would," he said. "When they wanted to

Discover Gold Eagle's power to keep you spellbound . . .

WITHOUT CHARGE OR OBLIGATION

Good books are hard to find. And hard men are good to find. We've got both.

Gold Eagle books are so good, so hard, so exciting that we guarantee they'll keep you riveted to your chair until their fiery conclusion.

That's because you don't just read a Gold Eagle novel . . . you *live* it.

Your blood will race as you join *Mack Bolan* and his high-powered combat squads—*Able Team, Phoenix Force, Vietnam: Ground Zero* and *SOBs*—in their relentless crusade against worldwide terror. You'll feel the pressure build page after page until the nonstop action explodes in a high-voltage climax of vengeance and retribution against mankind's most treacherous criminals.

Get 4 electrifying novels— FREE

To prove Gold Eagle delivers the most pulse-pounding, pressure-packed action reading ever published, we'll send you

4 novels— ABSOLUTELY FREE.

If you like them, we'll send you 6 brand-new books every other month to preview. Always before they're available in stores. Always at a hefty saving off the retail price. Always with the right to cancel and owe nothing.

As a Gold Eagle subscriber, you'll also receive . . .
- our free newsletter, AUTOMAG, with each shipment
- special books to preview free and buy at a deep discount

Get a digital watch— FREE

Return the attached Card today, and we'll also send you a digital quartz calendar watch FREE. It comes complete with a long-life battery and a one-year warranty.
Like the 4 free books, it's yours to keep even if you never buy another Gold Eagle book.

RUSH YOUR ORDER TO US TODAY

YOU CAN'T PUT
A GOOD BOOK DOWN

Razor-edged stories ripped from today's
headlines. Page-crackling tension. Spine-
chilling adventure. Adrenaline-pumping
excitement. Do-or-die heroes. Gold Eagle
books slam home raw action the way you
want it—hard, fast and real.

drum you out of the service, I took your side, I put myself on the line for you and gave you a job, gave you respectability again. And this is how you repay me!"

Jamison frowned at him. "You let them bust me down to second looey, then kept me down, kept me out of the sky. No big favor, thank you."

Wentworth threw the printout on the desk. "What are you doing here?" he asked.

"I haven't done anything, Marty," he said. "Don't get worked up about it."

"I'll get as worked up as I want to... Captain," Wentworth said. "I want you and all your men confined to quarters while I put together a case and find some space in the stockade. You're through. It's over."

"Well, Marty, you're partially right," Jamison said. "It is over—but not for me."

He pulled open his top desk drawer and took out the Beretta that lay there. Smiling, he pointed it at the general's chest and fired three times. Wentworth fell to the floor without a word and wheezed his last breath before his muscles relaxed for the last time.

Jamison picked up the telephone and dialed the extension to the front gate. He didn't need a lot of time, just another couple of days until he collected Stateside and disappeared forever.

"Security," came the voice on the other end of the line.

"Yeah," Jamison said. "O'Brian?"

"Yes, sir."

"You got anybody on the civilian?"

"Yes, sir. Jeffries is in pursuit."

"You'd better kill him this time, or it's your ass."

"Yes, sir."

"Look, we've got another problem. Your friend had a talk with Wentworth, and I had to take care of him."

"The general…you mean, like, you took *care* of the general?"

"Yeah, but I've got an idea. Get over here with a couple of your men and help me. I think we can kill two birds with one stone."

He hung up, regretting somewhat what would happen next. The fortunes of war, he supposed. He stuck the Beretta into his pants, then slipped his dress jacket on to cover it. O'Brian and his men arrived after only a few minutes.

"Stay here," he told the men who stared in disbelief at the body on the floor. "Don't let anybody in. We're going to have to move him in a few minutes."

"Why not now?" O'Brian asked.

"You'll see. You got the phone number on the cop?"

"Sure."

"Good. We'll need it."

He left then, walking the long block to Wentworth's office. Becky Davis was sitting at her desk when he walked in.

"Hank?" she said. "Is everything okay?"

He smiled. "Everything's fine," he said. "I told you it was just a misunderstanding."

"The general . . ."

"He'll be here in a few minutes."

She jumped up from behind the desk and ran to him, fitting easily into his arms. "Oh, Hank, I was so worried," she said.

"I'm like a cat," he said, his hands rubbing her back. "I always land on my feet." He kissed her on the neck, smelling the shampoo in her hair. And as she put her arms around him, he reached into his jacket pocket and brought out the automatic.

One hand went to her throat, pushing her a distance from him. He put the gun to her forehead and shrugged, smiling into her wide eyes. "Sorry, Becky." He pulled the trigger, splattering her brains all over the office wall.

10

Bolan drove along the coast highway, moving back in the direction of Hashi-san's home on Lake Ashi. The Mercedes was fast, a lot faster than the jeep that followed him, and he had to work to keep from pulling too far ahead. The road twisted like a snake, due to the nature of Honshu's oceanfront topography, and the white beaches were covered with people playing volleyball and swimming. It was desolation that he wanted, and there wasn't much to be found on an island the size of California with a population half that of the United States.

He'd call back and check with General Wentworth as soon as he had made some contact with the APs behind him. Bolan needed something concrete, something he could put his finger on that would straighten everything out and line it up in sequence. His frustration was dangerous, to him and to those close to him, and it was beginning to leave him frayed around the edges. His growing relationship with Junko, and her father's almost smothering approval of it, also left him with a dangerous uncertainty about himself and his place in the scheme of things. It wasn't a good way for him to be. He was the Executioner, the swift hand of justice. He needed to be sure of his feelings and his actions. If he was to survive this, he'd *have* to be sure of himself at all times.

Beginning now.

The Owakudani cutoff was just ahead. He made the sharp turn, the road grading upward almost immediately. He was heading for high, desolate ground—the almost prehistoric landscape of Mount Kamiyama.

The Mercedes hung low to the ground, taking the winding roads easily. Bolan stalked his prey by leading it, drawing it farther away from civilization and deeper into an isolated area. This he could understand. This he felt comfortable with.

He checked the rearview mirror. The APs were still behind him, hanging back. There were four of them in the jeep, four criminals trained by the United States government to kill, and right now he knew they wanted to kill Mack Bolan. The odds were hardly fair.

IT TOOK ICHIRO twenty minutes to get through the Yokota front gate. The base had been sealed off—put under red alert—as if it was wartime. Armored vehicles sporting M-60s prowled the grounds, manned by gunners in full battle dress. Even after Ichiro and Natsume were allowed to pass through the gate, they were held at the guard shack until the acting base commander, Colonel Murdock, came to meet them.

Murdock limped as he moved forward to greet them. His bad leg was the result of time spent in a Korean prisoner-of-war camp.

"Kendo," he said warmly, shaking hands with both men. "It's good to see you again."

"I'm sorry, Colonel, that it is under these circumstances," Ichiro replied.

Murdock nodded. He was drawn and pale, unsure of what to do. The colonel had been the civilian liaison, the Air Force equivalent of Ichiro, and as such had done a good job for a number of years. But that hardly prepared him to be thrust into a major policy-making role during an extreme emergency situation.

"It looks like a case of assassination," the colonel said. "But for the life of me, I can't figure out why."

"Can I see the death scene?"

"Certainly. Come with me."

They walked toward Base Ops, the series of offices Ichiro was always taken to when visiting the base to discuss incidents between airmen and civilians. There was a large crowd standing around General Wentworth's office.

They pushed through the crowd, and then Murdock turned to speak to Ichiro. "I'm going to put you onto Captain Jamison," the man said. "He saw the whole thing. Do you know him?"

"I've spoken to him on occasion about the conduct of his men," Ichiro replied, leaving out his personal dislike of the man.

The area outside Wentworth's office was roped off with yellow tape. APs stood guard within the perimeter. A captain stood near the stairs, smoking a cigarette and talking animatedly with another AP. Ichiro didn't need to ask Murdock if this was Jamison. He looked just as he sounded on the phone.

"Hank!" Murdock called, walking Ichiro and Natsume over to the man. "I have someone I'd like you to meet."

Jamison turned to them, and Ichiro recognized the man with him immediately. It was Sergeant O'Brian, who had given him so much trouble after the explosion at the pachinko parlor.

"Hank Jamison," the man said as he extended his hand.

"We've spoken before," Ichiro said, ignoring the outstretched hand.

"So we have," Jamison replied, the smile fading from his lips.

"What have you got?" Ichiro asked.

"Here's what I've pieced together," Jamison said, leading him up the short staircase to the office. "This civilian, name of . . . Reeves, comes in here early this afternoon. He presents his passport at the gate and is allowed inside."

"Reeves, did you say?" Ichiro asked.

"Yeah," O'Brian said from the bottom of the stairs. "The bastard you took away from me the other night. This wouldn't have happened if—"

"Easy," Jamison said, narrowing his eyes. "Anyway, this Reeves character walks over to this office. A few minutes later he leaves the base."

"Where do you come into all this?" Ichiro asked.

Jamison put his hand on the doorknob. "I was walking over here to have lunch with the general when I saw a civilian leaving. I didn't think much about it until I opened the door."

Jamison turned the knob and pushed the door open. A woman who might have been pretty once lay on the floor, arms and legs splayed, her head tilted to one side, eyes wide. The whole top of her head was missing.

Ichiro looked on with eyes accustomed to death, but that didn't stop him from experiencing a sick feeling in the pit of his stomach. A waste.

"Her name is Rebecca Davis," Jamison said. "She was a . . . friend."

"What did you do when you found her?" Ichiro asked.

"I probably should have called the gate right then to try and stop that guy, but I didn't. I ran in to the general's office to see if he was all right."

They moved to Wentworth's office. The general was sitting in his chair, slumped over the desktop as if he was asleep. Jamison walked to the body and lifted it slightly by pulling on the hair. The face had already turned gray, a grimace permanently etched across his mouth. The whole front of his uniform was soaked with blood that was already drying. Before Jamison settled the head back on the desk, Ichiro looked at its surface closely.

"This," Jamison said, pointing to the floor as he continued, "Is what I think we'll discover to be the murder weapon."

They all bent down and looked at a Beretta 92-SBF that had apparently been dropped on the floor. Bolan had carried a Beretta, but Ichiro wasn't sure that it was the same model. Even so, the 92-SBF had become standard issue for the U.S. Armed Forces, its availability highly probable on a base the size of Yokota.

He took a pen out of his pocket and stuck it through the trigger-guard. "Do you mind?" he asked, picking it up before the man could answer.

"As a matter of fact, I do," Jamison said, and Ichiro set the gun down immediately. "This is a problem for the Air Force to handle. You have no jurisdiction here."

"So sorry," Ichiro said as he got down on all fours and began searching the floor, Natsume getting down to help him.

"What are you doing?" Jamison asked.

"Looking for expended cartridges," Ichiro replied.

"I told you it's not your problem," Jamison said angrily. "What I want is for you to help us outside the gates. This man is loose on Japanese territory. Unless you mount a major manhunt and find him, your government is going to hear from my government and heads are going to roll, yours probably the first."

"I understand," Ichiro said.

"So go on and do it," Jamison snapped. "That bastard could be halfway to Osaka by now."

"Why do you think that this man killed General Wentworth?" Ichiro asked.

"Terrorist, most likely," Jamison said. "Wanted to disrupt the base...and he's done a pretty good job of it."

"Thanks for your time," Ichiro said and walked out of the room.

He didn't speak until he and Natsume were out of earshot and moving back toward the gate. "What do you think?" he asked the sergeant.

"Makes no sense," Natsume said. "No cartridges, hardly any blood on the desk..."

"I think he was killed somewhere else," Ichiro said, "and brought back to his office."

"What did you find on the gun?"

"The serial numbers had been filed off, not the Executioner's style. Neither was leaving the gun behind. And hadn't he been frisked at the gate coming in? That's common practice if one doesn't have a work permit."

"What are you going to do?" Natsume asked.

Ichiro looked at the ground. They had reached the gates and been waved through. His cruiser, with its lights flashing, was blocking a lane in front of the base. "I've got to put out an all-points bulletin for Mack Bolan," he said, climbing behind the wheel. "I can't hold it back any longer."

"They may say you've held it back too long," Natsume replied. "You could lose your job over this one."

"I figure to," Ichiro said and put the car in gear.

THE PINE AND LARCH FORESTS gave way to the black, chunky volcanic terrain of Kamiyama as the road wound up past the Chokoku-no-Mori, the Forest of Sculptures, where a number of the famous sculptors of the twentieth century had combined their work in a magnificent outdoor display. The road was precarious, a single lane etched out of the mountainside. Bolan was almost where he wanted to go—the cable car across Kamiyama.

It was early evening now, and most of the park area was closed. Bolan goosed the accelerator to put some distance between himself and the jeep as he covered the last kilometer of steep grade before pulling into the small parking area.

He climbed out of the car and ran to the edge of the lot, looking back down the mountain. He could see the jeep making its way up. Bolan knew that he had a couple of minutes.

A small bright red building with a gift shop attached housed the cable cars, which climbed straight up the mountainside to Owakudani, an active volcano that belched continuous streams of yellow sulphurous vapor into the hazy sky.

He ran up to the gift shop just as a young man with long hair and a tight red jacket was locking up.

"Do you speak English?" Bolan asked.

The boy rolled his eyes. "This tourist business, mister."

"I need to start the cable cars," Bolan said.

"We closed," the teenager said. "Come back tomorrow."

Bolan pulled a fistful of American money out of his pocket and showed it to the boy. "Do you know what this is?" he asked.

"You bet." The boy smiled widely and reached.

Bolan gave him half the money. "All you have to do is tell the four soldiers that will soon be here that I took the cable car up the mountain. Understand?" Bolan asked.

The boy was staring at the money in Bolan's hand. "Bait and switch," he said. "I understand, okay?"

"Okay," Bolan said. "Start a car up for me, will you?"

"No sweat."

Bolan could hear the jeep's engine whining up the hill. Just before it got to the parking lot, he slid under the Mercedes and lay on the cold ground.

The jeep squealed to a stop, blocking the Mercedes' exit, then Bolan saw jungle-booted feet running past his position. A quick exchange followed between the APs and the boy, then the airmen were in a gondola, heading up the mountain.

Bolan slid out from under the car and moved back to the boy, who sat by the turning gears that wound and unwound the cable. The boy smiled at the Executioner as he walked up. The car was already a hundred feet higher up the mountain.

"Domo arigato," the Executioner said and gave the boy the rest of the money. He noticed a lever near the boy's leg. "Does this shut it off?"

The smile faded, and the boy looked curious. He quickly showed Bolan the forward and reverse controls, plus the different uses for the levers.

"You'd better go," the Executioner said. "Have a safe trip home."

The boy left, and Bolan casually pulled the lever to jerk the machine to a halt. He looked up the mountainside; the gondola, its momentum stopped, was swinging back and forth on the wire.

Bolan shook his head. It was sure a lot easier to lose them than catch them. He reflected on the tough nature of Ichiro's job.

The Executioner walked back to the cars, taking a few minutes to go through the jeep to see if it would provide him with any information. The car itself was clean, but in the pocket of an airman's jacket, he found a rig—a syringe and spoon and small rubber hose used to mainline drugs. He also found a large packet of cocaine. These clowns not only pushed the poison, they used it.

A phone was ringing inside the cable housing. Whistling, Bolan walked back to the place and picked up the black receiver.

"You son of a bitch," the voice on the other end screamed. "You goddamned..."

Seconds later SMG fire rattled from the gondola, raking the building. Bolan pulled back a touch, avoiding it easily. He hung up the phone. Within a minute it rang again.

"I wonder," he said when he picked it up, "how long one of those cars can stay suspended in one place without straining and breaking the cables?"

"You son of—"

Bolan hung up again.

He looked up at the car dangling hundreds of feet above the sloping ground. A yellow fog surrounded it as the sky darkened. Bolan left the building to retrieve his shoulder harness from the trunk. He pulled Big Thunder out of its military webbing before returning to the office.

The phone rang again. He picked it up.

"What do you want?" the voice asked.

"Who am I speaking to?" Bolan replied.

"This is...Jeffries. What do you want?" The strain he was under was evident in his tone.

"I wonder if my .44 slugs will go through the walls of your cable car?" Bolan asked.

"No, don't..."

Bolan set the phone down and sighted up at the still swinging car through the open windows. He had a good view of two sides and most of the bottom. The Executioner aimed at the bottom and squeezed off a round. Within seconds he was answered by the rattle of handguns and automatic fire. It died down quickly and Bolan returned to the phone.

"You guys shoot off your ammo like you've got a bunch of it," he said. "I guess my shot must have gone through, though."

There was no answer.

"Now if you don't tell me, I'll just have to try another."

"No, no. It went through, you asshole, all right?"

Bolan waited a few seconds, then fired at the gondola, the shot ringing out through the mountains. Then he fired another round. Bolan thought he heard a scream in the dying echoes of the shot.

The phone rang again. Bolan picked it up. "Hello?"

Jeffries was breathing hard. "All right," he rasped. "What do you want?"

"Tell me everything you know about Operation Snowflake and tell me now," Bolan said.

"Captain Jamison set up this deal a couple of years ago with the Sonnojoi. I think he gambled a lot and got hooked up with these people through the Yakuza." Jeffries stopped, taking a ragged breath before continuing. "He spent a few months getting us out of jail and setting us up as APs so that we could help him."

"Help him how?"

"Dirty work," Jeffries said. "We do pickup and delivery work, maybe shoot a few scabs, stir up a little political trouble in our own way. We also smuggle arms off the base for the Sonnojoi to use. All of it lowers our price on the coke.''

''What about the cocaine?''

''We don't take that onto the base. We park it at a roadside and leave it with Jamison and O'Brian.''

''How does it get onto the base?''

''I don't know. They don't trust us to know that part. We load it up when the time comes and ship it out. They don't want us slicing any of it off for ourselves, I guess.''

Bolan laughed. ''They don't want you shooting your mouth off about where it is,'' he said. ''What about Dr. Lawrence Norwood? How does he figure in all this?''

''Who's he?''

Bolan leaned out the opening and fired at the gondola.

''I swear to God!'' Jeffries screamed. ''I swear I don't know!''

''What about the night at the pachinko parlor?''

''We were told to take out any Americans that were there. That's all, I swear!''

Bolan gazed up at the gondola in perplexity. All this jibed with the story Prine had told him. It was like a puzzle, with each man knowing only his piece. Jamison ran a tight, careful ship.

''How long is the operation going to run?'' Bolan asked.

''The heat's on,'' Jeffries replied. ''The captain had a meeting yesterday and told us we were making one big score and backing off for good. It's all supposed to go out tomorrow night.''

"How?"

"Two KC-135s are taking used equipment back to salvage in the States. We're putting the stuff on board and getting out with it. Captain Jamison has our orders set and everything.''

"You believe that?" Bolan asked. "You really think he'd take all of you out with him?"

"He's our captain," the man said with ruffled pride. "You gonna let us down now?"

"How many people have you killed, Jeffries?" Bolan asked. "Between the four of you, how many people have you killed for Captain Jamison?"

"I dunno," The man said. "Fifteen. Twenty."

"And how many people do you figure are hooked on or dead because of the poison you send back to the States?"

"Hey, it's just coke, you know?"

"Yeah," Bolan said. "I know."

He hung up the phone and went back to the jeep. He took out the rig he'd found in there and opened it, removing the syringe. The jeep had an extra five-gallon tank of gas attached to its back. He stuck the needle into the container and sucked out a syringeful of gasoline.

He moved to the front of the jeep and injected the gas into the tire on the driver's tire. Then he got into the jeep and eased it out of gear, letting it roll back a couple of feet so that he could back out the Mercedes.

The phone was ringing when he went back into the building. Instead of answering it, he put the machine in reverse and cranked it up. The gondola shook to a start and came back down the mountain.

He walked slowly back to the Mercedes and drove away. He had hard info for Wentworth now, enough to stop those planes and to lock up Jamison and his bunch. Dr. Norwood and his hydrogen bombs were still a mystery, but perhaps subsequent investigation would clear that up.

He was nearly a mile down the hill when he heard the roar of the jeep hurrying to catch him. The downgrade was steep, and it was possible to build up quite a bit of speed coming down. He found a shoulder that afforded a good view back up the hill and pulled over to watch.

The jeep kept coming, closing on him. A quarter of a mile away the tires had heated up sufficiently for the gas to explode in a burst of spontaneous combustion. The jeep jumped, then rolled off the road, careening down the mountainside with the rending of metal and a trail of fire.

Bolan watched it hit bottom far below him, then pulled back onto the road and headed off toward Hashi-san's dwelling, thinking of how he'd brought his own brand of reality to the serenity he had viewed that morning.

11

The rain had started again. It came hard this time, as if making up for the day's dry spell. Kendo Ichiro stood looking out the window of Tokyo Police Administration, watching it wash the skyscrapers and wondering what he'd do for a living once Commissioner Kawabata got through with him.

"Let me understand this, Lieutenant," Kawabata said from behind his desk, his eyes occasionally drifting to the sumo wrestling matches on the small TV set that sat before him. "You captured a dangerous international terrorist, let him walk away from your jail, had information that tied him to a gunfight on the highway, an explosion at Fuji, the murders of American military personnel at a nightclub and the destruction of a factory, yet you never put out a major alert on this man until after he committed the cold-blooded murder of the American commander of a military base."

"Yes, sir."

"And on top of that, you've been conferring with him **by** telephone and, in fact, shut down the entire subway system at great expense and nuisance to the

city in order to check out a lead this terrorist gave
you."

"Yes, sir." Ichiro turned from the window and
walked around to sit on the chair he had pulled up by
the desk.

Kawabata stared at him. The commissioner was a
political appointee who understood very little about
the guts of police work and its intuitive nature.

"Give me a reason why I shouldn't ask for your
badge and gun right now," he said.

Ichiro looked the man in the eye and saw no warmth
there. "I didn't just let him walk out of my jail," he
said. "Uniformed police came and set him free with
an authorization that was signed by you, Commissioner. The...terrorist, as you call him, has only gone
after criminals."

"It has not been proven that the Sonnojoi are
criminals."

"All right. He had good evidence about the explosion on Fuji and I followed through with him, hoping
to find Dr. Norwood."

Kawabata took off his glasses and rubbed his eyes.
"The radiation found at the site of the explosion is
hardly what I'd call overwhelming evidence. Now if he
had produced Dr. Norwood..."

"He says Dr. Norwood is suffering from severe radiation poisoning."

The commissioner turned his head and watched the
contest on television. "More speculation."

Ichiro leaned up against the desk. "And I don't think that Bolan had anything to do with the death of General Wentworth. I think it's all a part of this Operation Snowflake."

"And more speculation!" Kawabata said angrily. He slammed a hand down on the desktop. "This is ludicrous, Ichiro. Absolute fantasy. You used to be a good, solid professional, and now..." The man shook his head and put his glasses back on. "I'm sorry for you, Ichiro, and I'm most especially sorry for your family. But I can't have a man on my force who operates with the criminal element. Effective right now, you are suspended indefinitely. When the board of inquiry is held, I will vote that the suspension be made permanent." He pointed to the desktop. "You may leave your shield and weapon here."

Ichiro looked at the floor, humiliated. He unsnapped the holster from his belt and put his .38 service revolver on the desk. He took out his wallet, taking a last look at his lieutenant's badge before dropping it on top of the gun.

"Now that I'm a civilian," Ichiro said, "I can tell you exactly what I think of you."

He was interrupted by a sharp knock on the door.

"Just a minute!" Kawabata called, his eyes narrowing to angry slits.

The knocking came again, more persistent.

"What is it!" the commissioner practically screamed.

The door burst open, and Natsume poked his head inside. His eyes went immediately to the desk, taking the whole scene in at a glance. His eyes jumped to Ichiro, then to Kawabata.

"The body of Dr. Lawrence Norwood has just been found," he said. "On the Nishi-Ginza, near Yokota Air Base."

Kawabata stood slowly, and Ichiro could almost see the gears turning inside his head. "What was the cause of death, Sergeant?" the commissioner asked.

"They're doing an autopsy now," the man answered. "But unofficially the cause of death is kidney failure due to acute radiation poisoning."

Kawabata looked at Ichiro, his face an unreadable mask. Ichiro decided to push his hand.

"I guess I'll be leaving now," he said. "Since I no longer work for the department, I suppose I'll be able to tell the newspapers the truth about my suspension."

"Wait!" Kawabata said to Ichiro's retreating back.

The lieutenant stopped walking and winked at Natsume.

"I'll wait outside," the sergeant said, moving out of the office and shutting the door behind him.

Ichiro turned to face the man. "Yes?"

Kawabata sat down, his lips twisting as if not wanting to say the words. "Perhaps I was . . . premature in suspending you," he said.

"Is that an apology?" Ichiro replied.

"For you it is another chance. I'll make a wager with you, Lieutenant. You're so sure that you're on to something that I'll give you the chance to prove it." He reached out and slid the gun and badge closer to Ichiro. "I'll wager you twenty-four more hours against your career. If you want, you have one more day to prove your theories, twenty-four hours to either make it or break it. If you have put all of this together by tomorrow midnight, you walk away clean, no hearings, no newspapers."

"That's not much of a wager," Ichiro said.

"It's all I'm offering today," Kawabata replied. "Take it or leave it."

It was no contest. Ichiro would have promised the moon to clear his name and honor. He picked up the badge and gun and moved toward the door, turning as he opened it. "I don't like you any more than you like me," he said. "I'm going to do my best to shove this case right down your throat."

With that he strode out of the office into the agitated clerical complex of the administration building. Natsume jumped up off a chair he'd been sitting on near Kawabata's door and walked with Ichiro.

"Looks like I was just in time," the sergeant said.

"Yeah, but what happens when he finds out you were just making it up?" Ichiro replied, snapping the holster back onto his belt.

"That's the incredible part," Natsume said. "I didn't make it up!"

Ichiro stopped walking and stared at the man. "This means Bolan's right about everything. And if he's right, it's all coming to a head soon."

"What do we do?" Natsume asked.

Ichiro put his shield back in his wallet. "First, I call my wife and tell her I won't be home. Second, we redouble our efforts to catch Bolan. I need him badly right now. Finally, we find the Sonnojoi. Isn't there a demonstration scheduled tonight?"

"*Hai*. At Tachikowa."

"Good. We'll arrest some, no matter what it takes. One thing I've learned from Mr. Bolan is that sometimes the law just gets in the way of what is right."

"Is it too noisy for you?" Junko yelled across the table to Bolan.

The big man smiled, shaking his head. The bar was mobbed, which made it easier to remain unseen. Between the people singing at the tables and the vocal group cheering on the sumo wrestlers on the television in the corner, Bolan felt more closed in than he felt on a New York subway at rush hour. He shouldn't have been out in public, sitting in one place, but he couldn't help it. He wanted to spend time with Junko, get to know her as something other than a fellow warrior. It was her who had recommended this place, a cross between Japanese and American culture, featuring the food of both countries and impromptu songfests.

He was at a loss about what to do next. For reasons beyond him, the phone lines to Yokota Air Base were cut off, as was the number General Wentworth had given him. Something was up, but he hadn't had a chance to find out what. Without Wentworth he wasn't sure how to proceed. Unless Hashi-san was able to help him find the organizational meeting places of the Sonnojoi, he could very well end up losing the ball in the last minutes of the game.

"You seem distant," Junko said. Tonight she was dressed as a Westerner in a summer skirt and blouse.

"I'm sorry," he said. "Guess I never get too far away from business."

She reached across the table and took his hands. "It's all right," she said. "This thing with the Sonnojoi has been a continual nightmare for me since my brother died. To you, it is the immediate danger. Perhaps my own senses have become dulled."

He took a small sip from the *ochoko* of sake that sat before him. "The Sonnojoi is, unfortunately, only a part of my problem. If I can't stop that shipment tomorrow night, tons of cocaine will flood American bases within a day. And for some reason the whole base seems to be sealed off."

A small stage was set off to one side. People in the bar took turns going up to the microphone and singing. It was part of the deal. An Australian soldier had climbed up on stage and had begun to sing "Waltzing Matilda" in a loud, off-key voice.

"I'm sorry to add to your troubles," Junko said, eyes downcast.

"What do you mean?"

"I heard my father this morning...pushing me at you."

He reached across the table and took her hands in his. "Nobody has to push us together," he said. "I feel a kinship with you that runs deep, deeper than I knew I was still capable of."

"We understand one another," she replied simply.

"And accept."

She nodded, smiling. "I'm glad my father approves of you."

He sat back in his chair and stared at her, her physical perfection marred only slightly by the small bandage on her face from a glass cut of the night before. "So am I," he said, and for just a second he allowed himself to be something other than the Executioner.

Screams came from around the TV—someone had won a sumo match, and money was changing hands between the betters at the bar.

"Your father is a singular sort of human being," Bolan said. "His dedication to his cause is almost frightening."

"That's his Bushido code," she answered, drinking down a small cup of sake warmed to body temperature. "It controls every aspect of his life."

"Did the adherence to the code begin with the death of your brother?"

She shook her head. "He's practiced it for as long as I can remember. He simply applied it aggressively to his business before that."

"To what end?" Bolan asked, confused.

"To uphold family honor," she replied, then spoke again when she saw the question in his face. "I'm not sure of all this myself, but I think it goes back to the great war. My father's family came from Nagasaki. They were a proud and strong and powerful family, claiming ties all the way back to Asano and the forty-seven *ronin*. My father was rebellious and disregarded the family heritage. When the war came, he ran off to the mountains to live as a hermit rather than fight to uphold the honor of Japan and of the family...."

She looked at him, sighing loudly. "I'm probably boring you. I'm sorry."

"No, go on," Bolan said.

She shrugged. "There's not much more. Hashi-san came down out of the mountains to find that the city of his birth was no more, that his city, his family, his friends, all the things he had known and loved, had been vaporized in a instant by an atomic bomb."

"And he felt guilty," Bolan said.

She nodded. "Of all that had died, he felt that he was most deserving of death. He adopted the Bushido code then, diligently rebuilding his country to its former greatness."

"Does he hate Americans for it?"

"You see how he treats you," she said. "Does he hate you?"

"No," he said, then thought a minute. "A man once told me that there is a great deal of difference between honor and duty. I think I'm beginning to understand something of what he said."

The Aussie had completed his singing to raucous applause. He tried to walk but fell off the stage near Bolan's table. Bolan reached down to help him up.

"Thanks, mate," the man said, standing shakily to readjust his fatigues.

"Mack!" Junko called, laughing, and Bolan turned to see her being led, protesting, toward the stage. It was her turn.

People around him were clapping their approval, Bolan joining in the applause. "Go on!" he yelled.

She rolled her eyes, smiling wide, and allowed herself to be hoisted onto the stage as the spotlight picked her out. She began to sing, a small, sad song, her voice tentative at first, then gaining strength. Bolan wished he could understand the Japanese lyrics.

"Mind if I sit for a minute, mate?" the Aussie asked him, pointing to Junko's empty chair.

"Take a load off," Bolan said.

The man sank down. "Thanks. Lost me own place at the bar when I went to sing."

"A popular sport," Bolan said, referring to the sumo wrestling.

The Aussie nodded. "I always say you can tell a country by its sports."

"What do you mean?"

"Okay," he said, leaning forward. "America has football, mean and aggressive, but with a lot of laws and rules. In England it's cricket, civilized and boring. Latin countries have soccer to cool their hot blood. Australians play rugby. It's untamed and without rules, like the outback. In Japan it's sumo wrestling, a sport of ceremony, no action, internal."

"Explain," Bolan asked, fascinated.

"I've lived in the Orient for years," the man said, slurring his words slightly. "I've never seen anything as devious as this sport. Sumo wrestling is a mind game. It consists of a long, traditional ceremony that either opponent can halt by simply performing a part of the ceremony wrong. At that point the whole thing starts again. They will do this over and over, as each player tries to wear down the other's mental vigilance. If both players let the ceremony go to its natural conclusion, the contest is over in seconds. Physical strength is the given. The mental game is the whole thing."

"And you think this mirrors the Japanese mind?"

"Absolutely. Everything takes place under the surface. Face must be maintained, honor upheld. It ain't so much what you do but how you do it."

Bolan thought about that, his mind dwelling on the intricate puzzle that he was involved with. Perhaps he was concentrating too much on what was going on at the surface level. Perhaps the answers lay on a deeper, more internal plane.

"Let me ask you a question," Bolan said. "How come you're the only uniform I see out here so soon after payday?"

The man laughed. "You mean you haven't heard? Some American chap blew away the Yokota base commander and his secretary earlier today. They've put both Yokota and Tachi under red alert and canceled all off-base activities. I got out because I'm just here TDY and they really couldn't hold me. That's why I've had so much to drink. I'm drinking for all me mates tonight."

"Do they know who did it?"

"Sure. He didn't hide anything. The largest manhunt in Japanese history is being conducted to find him."

Damn. Jamison. He had no idea of the lengths that bastard would go to. The man was buying time, just trying to hold it together.

"The guy's probably halfway back to Russia or someplace by now," Bolan said, feeling the Aussie out.

The man shook his head. "The authorities think he's still in Japan. They been showing his picture on the telly all day. Fact is, mate, he looks . . . a lot . . . like . . . you."

With those words the Aussie's eyes got glassy, and he fell forward on the table, out cold. Bolan drew himself in. He shouldn't have allowed personal feelings to interfere while he was on a mission. Here he was, weapons in the car, out in the open in hostile territory. He'd have to get Junko and get out of there.

Just then the applause rose for Junko as she finished her song, laughing. Bolan stood to help her off the stage as people began pushing him up to take her place.

He turned to the crowd. "No, no," he said, waving his hands around, but Junko was pulling him up with her.

He feared resisting too much, not wanting to make a scene. How long could it take, a minute, two? He'd get it over with and get the hell out of there.

He climbed onto the stage to wild applause. The crowd was ready for anything at this point. He stood tentatively at the microphone, unable to remember a song. Then all at once the spotlight came on, blinding him.

As Bolan's eyes adjusted to the light, the front door opened, and uniformed police officers entered. The crowd was laughing and applauding, urging Bolan to begin.

The officers were moving through the bar, checking the patrons, getting closer to his position. "Everybody stand up!" Bolan called. "Let's all sing 'Take Me Out to the Ball Game.'"

The crowd was up, waving their hands in the air and singing the only American song that most baseball-happy Japanese knew.

Whistles were blowing as the cops charged the stage. Bolan glanced down to see Junko by his foot. He launched himself off the stage and with outstretched arms took out three of them at once.

He scrabbled to his feet, grabbed Junko's hand and charged toward the back of the place, knocking over tables as he ran. They hit the swinging kitchen door on a dead run, knocking over a waiter carrying a huge tray of sushi and hamburgers. Dishes flew everywhere, crashing loudly.

A small cook in a white T-shirt and apron began screaming at them. They hurried through the kitchen as he picked up a cleaver and came after them.

Out the back door a police cruiser was parked in the narrow alley with its lights flashing. Without slowing they jumped onto the hood of the car, then over the fence on the other side and down another winding street. Gunshots followed them.

The streets whirled crazily past them, and Bolan lost his bearings almost immediately. Everything was twisted, and Bolan knew the logic of it was internal, just like the sumo wrestling.

They turned, but police lights drove them back past rows of paper houses. Lights came on in many of the homes as sirens tore into the night. Another fork and more lights. They retraced their steps again, racing through rain and mud to another fork. This one led to a still, dark street.

"Can we make it back to the car?" Bolan called against the rain that was now falling quite heavily.

"Not from here!"

"You know this neighborhood?"

"Here!" She pointed down an alley that dead-ended at another tall fence. Whistles blew behind them. They took the alley. "My aunt lived in this area. She used to have a—"

Junko had stopped running and was moving slowly. Rain streamed down her face, and her clothes were wet and clinging. She had long since abandoned both shoes.

"She had a what?" Bolan asked.

The sirens seemed to be converging on their area. It would only be a matter of time if they didn't make a move soon.

"It's dark," she said. "It's been years, I—"

"She had a what?" Bolan asked again.

"There!" Junko said triumphantly, pointing up. "A tree house!"

"A tree house?" Bolan questioned.

LIEUTENANT ICHIRO SAT in the passenger's seat as Natsume drove toward the demonstration at Tachikowa Air Base. Demonstrations for the most part were civilized in Japan, with the protesters registering the times of their demonstrations with the police and scheduling them for everyone's convenience. Disruptions had only happened lately because of the Sonnojoi.

They pulled up to the fringe of the demonstration, just behind the barricades. Their headlights shone into the crowd of people, most of whom carried umbrellas. The dark, silent, Special Service vans were parked nearby.

"Have you talked to everybody?" Ichiro asked.

"They have all been sworn to secrecy," the sergeant replied.

"Nobody is to know about what I'm doing," Ichiro said. "I've got a few hours to wrap this up one way or the other, and nothing's going to hold me back or tie me down." He pulled his .38 out of its holster and checked the load.

"Kawabata is going to want reports on you, Kendo," Natsume said, watching the lieutenant reholster his weapon. "The secrecy is going to upset him."

"I'm done for, anyway. I'm not going to have him interfering with this." He opened his door. "Come on, let's go."

Natsume grabbed his arm and stopped him. "Are you sure you're doing the right thing?"

Ichiro looked at him hard. "What's the right thing?" he asked and pointed to his heart. "Down here, I'm doing the right thing. These animals have to be stopped. I'm going to stop them."

He moved out into the rain as Natsume called out the riot squad on the car radio. The crowds were chanting and shaking their umbrellas in the air, and Ichiro felt a rush of adrenaline. So much of police work was plodding and uneventful. Tonight he was taking to the street. Tonight he was going to deal out justice, and it felt good. It felt really good.

He walked the fringe of the crowd. The riot squad filed quietly out of the vans to follow him. They looked like medieval warriors with their shields, pikes and helmets.

Sergeant Noda approached Ichiro as he stood watching the crowd.

"Orders, sir?" Noda asked.

Ichiro turned to him. "The Sonnojoi are near the fence, Sergeant, as always. I want them isolated, I want them taken. We'll use whatever force is necessary to accomplish this."

"How much force—" the man began.

"Deadly force, Sergeant," Ichiro said. "These people are killers and terrorists. They are probably armed and extremely dangerous. You and your men have my permission to do whatever it takes to isolate and arrest them."

Sergeant Noda smiled through the rain-spotted visor of his helmet. "Yes, sir!" he said enthusiastically. "We await only your orders."

Ichiro felt Natsume at his arm. He turned to the man. "If you don't have the stomach for this, you may go now," he said.

The older man nodded slightly. "I was busting cheap Yakuza out of waterfront bars when you were still an infant," Natsume replied. "Just point me in the right direction and see what I do."

Ichiro smiled, patting his assistant on the arm. "Good," he said and turned to Noda. "At your order, Sergeant."

The man nodded, his face tightened now, instincts ready. He turned to his men and raised a fist in the air. "Let's go!" he called.

They waded into the crowd, Ichiro and Natsume right along with them. The demonstrators were suddenly surrounding them like floodwaters, but the waters broke and receded under their relentless push. Their pikes swung low, clearing a wide path, and within a minute they had fifteen Sonnojoi walled off from the rest of the demonstration.

The Sonnojoi, backs to the fence, trapped, stood facing the forces of law. Several seconds elapsed—a standoff—when all at once one of the punks lowered the sign he was carrying and a riot cop found himself looking down the barrel of a Remington .12-gauge pump shotgun.

The punk fired, but the shot deflected from the cop's body armor. It was the biggest mistake he'd ever make.

The cops charged, swinging high with their pikes. The punk with the shotgun lost his helmet to thrashing bamboo, then lost his life under a blast of Ichiro's .38 when he tried to pump and shoot again.

Cornered, the punks fought back viciously with fists and guns and knives. Ichiro's highly trained tactical squad responded with machinelike precision. They poked and slashed with the flexible poles, and black-suited punks fell like mown hay under the scythe.

Ichiro and Natsume, side by side, threw two men up against the fence. APs on the American side pushed the Sonnojoi back with their billy clubs when the punks tried to climb over.

Ichiro butted his man in the gut with the barrel of his .38, then ripped his helmet off when the man doubled over. The punk came at him with wild eyes. He was young, snarling like a vicious animal through clenched teeth.

All of the anger that had built up in Ichiro erupted. The lieutenant drew his arm back, and a weapon-filled fist drove into the man's face. The .38 barrel busted through the curtain of teeth to go down the punk's throat, gagging him.

The punk's hands went to his face, and Ichiro kicked him viciously in the groin, driving the screaming Sonnojoi to the pavement.

Ichiro turned to Natsume, who was delivering karate blows that dropped his man in a quaking pile on the ground. The two men shared a look, then they both went to their knees to handcuff their quarries.

Ichiro stood and looked around. Sonnojoi lay all over the ground, their faces bloody, their clothes slashed from the poles, long streams of blood pouring from the cuts. Two cops were down, but neither appeared seriously hurt.

"Haul them in!" Ichiro shouted into the rain. He was breathing heavily. "Take any ID you can from them, *any* ID. Start processing. Question them to get their background and information about their organization. Do what you have to do, but give me results by morning."

He turned to walk away, then spun back around. "They're animals," he spat, "treat them that way."

MACK BOLAN SAT on the hard floor of the tree house and watched Junko sleep. They were twenty feet in the air, on the strong cross limbs of a huge larch. The tree house itself was capped by a red pagoda roof that would be visible in the daytime but blended completely with its surroundings in the dark.

The local cops were persistent, he'd have to give them that. They'd been moving around Bolan's position for the better part of four hours, crossing and recrossing the pathway beneath the tree house, even looking up from time to time but never seeing them through the leafy branches.

The rain had settled to a soft drizzle that fell gently on the thatched roof, restful and hypnotic. It had finally gotten the better of Junko, and she'd curled up in the cramped space and gone to sleep, her head in his lap.

Designs, so many designs. Her head in his lap was close and loving, but it also served to keep him there. Whether she intended that to happen was probably a moot point. That he was thinking along those lines was, however, of tremendous importance.

He had begun to question his connection to Hashi-san. It didn't matter that the man loved and trusted him. It didn't matter how he felt about the man's daughter. The fact was that the Executioner was filtering all his thoughts and information through someone else, someone he barely knew. He had never operated this way before. Never. He had survived and succeeded by depending upon himself and a select few he had handpicked. Hashi-san was a beguiling, generous, trusting man—but was he trustworthy? It was a question Bolan had no answer for, and that bothered him.

He sat there in the black rainy night, stroking the hair of a woman he could love, and thought about internals. Hashi-san trusted Bolan not through instinct but because he had access to the Executioner's files and history. Mack Bolan was a man who lived his life up-front, his honesty on his sleeve. He wasn't hard to figure. You either had to take the Executioner the way he was or leave him alone. But Hashi-san was a game player. What did he actually know about the man?

He certainly wasn't the warrior he had presented himself to be. His motivation came through his guilt, guilt over the betrayal of his family honor during the Second World War, guilt over the death of his son. His honor sprang, then from external forces, not from deep internal commitment.

What else did he know about this modern, monetary Bushido warrior? He forced his daughter to live a double life in order to fulfill his emotional needs, yet didn't care for her much beyond his own wants. He seemed to be using her as chattel to bargain with Bolan, without a care for her own feelings. He had a mercenary on his payroll, a man whose commitment came only through money, something that a businessman like Hashi-san would understand but something that made Bolan's skin crawl.

Between Bolan and Hashi-san, the dealings had been fruitful, at least on the surface; but ever since talking to the Aussie, the Executioner had begun looking under the surface. What was really going on? How did the Sonnojoi know to find Bolan and Junko on the highway that day? How did they know where to find Dr. Norwood? He had no idea if or how Hashi-san could be involved with these things; he was simply trying to give the man credit for a mind capable of many thoughts.

When he had gone back to the man's house at Ashi after disposing of the APs at the cable car, he had been told by Hashi-san that no connection between the words on the bottom of the helicopter skid and a business could be made. All right. He'd start there. Instead of completely depending on the man, he'd initiate his own investigation into that possibility. If his suspicions were proven wrong, fine. He'd been wrong before, no harm done. But if the suspicions were correct...

He looked down at Junko, sleeping so peacefully. What was her connection to all of this? What would his doubts do to her? In many ways her world was as innocent and isolated as a child's. Her respect and trust for her father was certainly childlike, one of her most endearing qualities. He leaned over and kissed her lightly on the cheek. She stirred, smiling in her sleep, but didn't awaken.

12

Kendo Ichiro sat with his feet up on his desk, nursing his eighth cup of coffee and trying to make sense out of the scattered pieces of puzzle that were laid out before him in the form of pages of information. Outside, morning had broken, rainy and depressing. There seemed to be no end to it. His stomach hurt, and his wife, Mika, was angry at him for missing their son's piano recital the night before.

"We have quite a glamorous job, don't we?" Natsume said from the doorway. He shuffled in, his suit wrinkled and stained with coffee and blood, and placed two more sheets of paper on the desk.

"Anything?" Ichiro asked hopefully, sitting up and looking at the computer printouts.

"Of course," Natsume replied. "They've all confessed and given us the names and dates of every crooked dealing they've ever done."

"That is not very funny," Ichiro said.

"Sorry." Natsume sank heavily into his own chair, a deep sigh escaping his lips. "They all have the same basic story and they stick to it no matter what we do."

"I know," Ichiro said. "They have no formal meetings or hierarchy. They formed themselves at work through love of their native land and communicate by telephone. They've never performed any illegal actions and don't intend to perform any."

Natsume clapped his hands lightly. "You could join them yourself at this point."

Ichiro smiled dully. "Anything on Bolan?"

"They've given up the search," Natsume said, apologizing when Ichiro groaned. "They thought they had him last night, but he somehow managed to slip away."

Ichiro rubbed his eyes. "I wonder if *he* got any sleep?"

"What now?" Natsume asked. "Short of pulling out their fingernails, I'm not sure what else we can do to those punks in there. They're already screaming about their rights."

"Well, we've got plenty of cause to hold them," Ichiro began, "just from last night's trouble. Meanwhile, I've worked out a composite of the typical Sonnojoi member. Let me try it on you and see if we can find any weak links in their chain."

"Shoot."

Ichiro picked up the piece of paper that contained his synopsis of all the other pieces of paper on his desk. It wasn't much, but it was all he had to go on. "The typical Sonnojoi," he read, "is male, nineteen to twenty-five years of age. He's idealistic and impressionable, with no record of prior criminal offenses. He's doggedly loyal and more than willing to die for his cause. He lives with his family but is secretive enough to keep his affiliation with his political groups to himself. He works in a blue-collar job and is highly regarded at the workplace. He works for either the Asano Corporation in their steel mill, the Hoji-Honshu Trucking Company, the Blue Star Aircraft Parts and Material Company, or Genji Produce as a boxcar loader. He has a rigid code of ethics and conduct. He's quiet and undemonstrative. He has no wife or female friends.''

"Almost like a warrior class," Natsume said.

"We have no warrior class," Ichiro returned. "Anything else strike you?"

Natsume laid his head on the desk. "Nothing outside the geography," he said softly.

"What do you mean?"

The sergeant sat up, grabbing a bottle of antacid off his desk. "Years ago," he began, popping several tablets into his mouth, "when I drove a squad car for a living, the area around the steel mills was my beat. Now I'm not sure about the produce company, but the other businesses you mentioned are all grouped within several square miles of the Yokota and Tachikowa Air Bases."

Ichiro stood, walking to a huge wall map of the Tokyo area. He moved to the section of the map containing the bases and stared at them.

"Do me a favor," he said, continuing to stare. "Get out a phone book and look up Genji Produce for me. Let's see where it is."

Natsume rummaged through his desk and got out a tattered telephone directory. Ichiro listened to the pages rustling behind him as he kept watching, trying to stop his brain on the point of intersection with the information on the map.

"Got it," Natsume said. "Genji Produce is less than a mile from the trucking company."

Suddenly Ichiro began backing slowly away from the map. "I've got it," he whispered.

"What? What is it?"

"Chikatetsu!" Ichiro yelled. *"Chikatetsu!* I think I know what it is!"

"What?"

"No time now," Ichiro said, grabbing his sports jacket off the back of his chair and moving toward the door. "I've got a job for you. Look up all those businesses. Find out all about them—how long they've been there, who owns them—just do a work-up for me."

He opened the door.

"Where are you going?" Natsume asked.

"The library."

"It's closed this early."

Ichiro walked out the door, then poked his head in again. "We're cops, remember? We can make them open it."

MACK BOLAN STOOD at the pay phone in the gift shop, trying to balance the phone on his shoulder while studying the huge volume of kanji script translations in his hands.

"What the hell did you do over there?" Hal Brognola asked, his voice sleepy and distant. "Everybody up to and including the joint chiefs are going nuts over this Yokota thing."

"It wasn't me," Bolan said. "Wentworth confronted Jamison with information about Operation Snowflake. Jamison killed him and blamed it on me."

"The end result's the same, though, isn't it?" Brognola asked.

"What do you mean?"

"I mean, Jamison's sealed in tight, in control. He can frame you all he wants. You're odd man out, Mack."

Bolan paged through the huge, hard-bound book. Kanji is a complex form of character writing adopted from the Chinese and containing over thirty thousand characters. More were added all the time through *katakana*, a shorthand process used to merge Western words into the Japanese system.

"What about making things happen on your end?" Bolan asked.

"I checked before I left the office tonight," Hal said. "We've got an investigating team going over there, but they won't arrive until tomorrow. Any word sent from here will only get filtered through Jamison's system. If I step forward—"

"Don't do that," Bolan interrupted. "That will only tie you to me. I wouldn't wish that on anybody right now."

"Do you know when the coke's going out?" Brognola asked.

"Tonight," Bolan said. "On two KC-135s."

"I can probably arrange to search those planes when they arrive in the States."

"Yeah," Bolan said, stopping at the characters for snow in his book. "*If* they even land in the States. Jamison is logged out on one of those planes himself. God only knows where he'll land them now that the heat's on."

"If he wants to sell the stuff, he'll still have to work through his contacts."

Bolan grunted, his finger running down the page of American words and their kanji counterparts. "Maybe," he said. "There's something else, Hal."

"What?"

"The two hydrogen bombs that the Sonnojoi forced Dr. Norwood to make. I have no idea where they are. In fact, I'm not convinced that Jamison isn't all tied up with them somehow."

"What would anyone want with—"

"To blow something up, Hal," Bolan said. "You don't make atomic weapons just for fun. The Sonnojoi or Jamison or both intend to do something with those bombs."

"What are you going to do?"

"Find the coke and find the bombs before the Air Force, the Sonnojoi and the Tokyo Police find me."

"Sounds like your dance card's full."

"I'm a popular guy," Bolan returned. "You keep an eye out for those planes, Hal."

"Mack, I . . ."

"Save it, Hal. Words just get in the way."

Bolan hung up the phone, angry at the corner he'd boxed himself into. He'd assumed that Wentworth could take care of himself, and now he was paying the price for that assumption.

Bolan leaned against the inside of the booth for a minute, looking out at the shelves full of knickknacks and Japanese china that filled the small store. In the book his finger still rested on the kanji for snowflake. They were nothing like the characters he had found on the skid of the Huey. Nothing like that all.

Hashi-san had lied to him.

He closed the book and moved away from the phone. This changed everything. Where Hashimoto and Junko stood or what their game was, he didn't know. All he was sure of was that he could trust no one but himself at this point, something he should have known from the beginning.

He moved to the counter to pay for the dictionary, and the woman who ran the store figured the price on an abacus. On impulse Bolan once again wrote down the characters he had seen on the helicopter and shoved them in front of the gray-haired woman.

"Can you read this?" he asked.

She narrowed her eyes, then put on bifocals and held the paper out at arm's length. "You kanji very bad," she said.

"So I've been told."

She set the paper down on the countertop, her fingers pointing to the first of the characters. "This say... maybe company, like business. This say Asano, very famous hero to Japanese."

Bolan felt a hard knot in the pit of his stomach. He pointed to the first set of characters again. "Could this be... corporation?"

"*Hai*... corporation. Yes, that's right."

"Thanks." Bolan replied, sick at heart.

"Do itashimashite," the woman responded, making change for the thousand-yen note Bolan had laid on the counter.

He moved out of the gift shop into the drizzle of the early afternoon. When he and Junko had escaped the tree house and gotten back to her car, she had driven him to his place and then hurried off on business for her father. Despite the danger he had walked up to the complex of shops near the base to set his mind at rest. He had accomplished just exactly the opposite.

This revelation made absolutely no sense to him. He had fought the Sonnojoi for Hashi-san, had killed them for him. They had attacked his own daughter viciously. At every step the old man had shown his hatred for the organization. It made no sense that he could be involved with it.

There was another possibility. The helicopter could have been stolen and repainted. The only reason the stencil was left on the bottom of the skid was because no one would see it. That made sense to Bolan, except for one thing, the thing that had nagged him from the start—the only people he had mentioned Fujikyu to were Junko and Hashi-san.

He used the shadows and the alleyways to work his way back to the "safe" house. The first thing he was going to do was gather the few belongings he had picked up since staying there, then quickly find another place to stay. After that it would be time to have a talk with his benefactor, preferably in a controlled situation. It was all up for grabs now. He had trusted and been used in return. He wouldn't make that mistake again.

And through it all one small thought kept filtering into his mind. Hashi-san could have killed him or had him killed a dozen times in the course of the past several days. Hell, he could have left him in Ichiro's jail. But he hadn't. He had freed him instead and treated him like a son. Why?

He walked through the muddy streets of his neighborhood, turning the corner that led to his house. He took no more than five paces before the hairs stood up on the back of his neck. Everything looked normal, placid, but something wasn't right. He turned to run, but three punks in black leather jumped out of the bushes to block his way with their shotguns. He heard them then, all around him.

He turned in a slow circle. Shotguns were pointed at him from windows and doorways, from behind trees and shrubs. They were everywhere. His house was "safe" because it was located in a neighborhood of Sonnojoi.

He stood with his arms up. The kanji dictionary lay forgotten in the mud at his feet. His front door opened, and Dr. Mett slowly walked out. The man wore a white suit, and galoshes covered his shoes because of the mud.

Mett walked down the short entry path and stood by the street, his face, as usual, showing no emotion. He and Bolan shared a look. The Executioner's mind desperately searched for a way out, but he knew there was none.

Dr. Mett pulled a pistol out of his jacket. It looked like a gas-powered sports pistol. He raised it slowly, aiming high. "Goodbye, Mr. Bolan," he said and pulled the trigger.

Bolan heard the sound, felt the flare of pain in his head. Then he whirled steadily downward into the calmest, blackest night.

13

"I see no reason why we should have to remain sealed off like this," Colonel Murdock said as he and Jamison sat at the bar in the Officers' Club. "It was an isolated incident. I just can't believe it could be tied to anything larger."

"Drink up, Charlie," Jamison said, patting the acting base commander on the back. "Think about it. There was violence at Tachi last night. Troubles are escalating. This man they call the Executioner has been involved in terrorist activities all over the world. Don't tell me the incident is isolated."

"I don't know," Murdock said, finishing his third Scotch and water of the day. "At the Pentagon they told me to use my own discretion until the investigating team arrives. I just don't see—"

"Listen," Jamison said. "Security is my job, right? Why don't you just let me do what I'm an expert at? That's what I get paid for." He motioned toward the bartender. "Another Scotch here."

Murdock put a hand over his glass. "I think I've had enough."

"Ah, come on, Charlie," Jamison said, smiling. "You've got Wentworth's job now. You've got to learn to drink like him."

"All right." The man sighed. "Just one more."

"That's the ticket. You've got enough on your mind just running the base. You let me take care of all the details on this assassination thing, and it'll all be over before we know it."

Murdock nodded, his eyes half closed. "Thanks, Hank. I can't tell you how much I appreciate this."

Jamison heard the front door open and saw O'Brian poking his head in, trying to adjust his eyes to the low lighting.

"One of my men," Jamison said, pointing toward the door. "Duty calls."

Murdock nodded. "Thanks for the talk, Hank," he said.

Jamison patted his back again. "You just leave all the worrying to me."

"With pleasure. I never wanted this job to begin with, and I like it less with each passing minute."

Jamison threw a twenty on the bar to cover the tab, then walked to the front door, moving out with O'Brian.

"Any problems with Murdock?" O'Brian asked as they walked out into the rain.

Jamison shook his head. "He's a candy ass. I think he'd rather eat Drano than make a decision. Come on. Drive me over to the flight line."

They climbed into O'Brian's jeep. "They found Jeffries a little while ago," the sergeant said, putting the jeep into gear and taking off.

"And?"

"He and the others were at the bottom of a mountain—dead."

"Damn!" Jamison pounded the door panel with his fist. He sat quietly for a minute. "I'm not happy with this, O'Brian. I'm not happy with *you*."

O'Brian turned to stare at him, his face drained of color. "The guy's froze out. There's no way he can…"

"There had better not be," Jamison said quietly.

They pulled up to the flight line and stopped, and Jamison climbed out to stand beside the vehicle. In the distance two huge planes were being loaded with legitimate equipment.

"All I want is eight hours. In eight hours we'll be out of here and gone with the goods. Then I don't care what the son of a bitch does."

"Eight hours, no sweat," O'Brian said, smiling at Jamison. But the man refused to return his look.

LIEUTENANT KENDO ICHIRO MOVED into the squad room with a load of books under his arm. His face was drained and puffy from lack of sleep, his hair obviously uncombed. He dropped the books on his desk and stared at Yukio Natsume, who sat slowly eating a bowl of *ramen*. His chopsticks worked methodically, his eyes were nearly closed.

"Your wife called," Natsume said. "Fifteen times."

"Never mind that," Ichiro said, picking up a large volume and carrying it to the man's desk. "Look at this."

He opened the book to a two-page spread of a blueprint for a huge underground complex of hangars and barracks. *"Chikatetsu,"* he said, pointing to the blueprints.

Natsume set his bowl down and opened his eyes wide. "I'd forgotten," he said. "It's been so many years."

Ichiro turned the page of the history book, a plethora of still photographs filling the facing pages. "During the war we fought successfully in tunnels on South Pacific islands against the U.S. Navy. When it became obvious that we were losing the war and would soon be fighting on our own soil, our generals concocted a bold plan," he recounted.

Natsume nodded, wiping his mouth on a napkin. "I should have remembered this," he said. "I was around then. They began constructing a series of tunnels between Yokota and Tachikowa. The idea was that we could house our Air Force and our troops down there and make them immune to American bombers, which were at that time causing a great deal of havoc."

"Right," Ichiro said. "It would probably have been successful, except that Hiroshima was bombed, then Nagasaki, and the war was over within a week. The tunnels were never completed. When the U.S. government took possession of the bases, they simply ordered the tunnels sealed because of a large number of booby traps blocking the entrances. They intended to go back in and clean out the tunnels, but soon enough they were forgotten and have remained unexplored until this day.''

Natsume bent and looked closely at the old black-and-white photos in the book. The tunnels were mammoth. There were large hangars containing many squadrons of Zeroes, stored wing-to-wing. There were armories and mess halls and large barracks. ''A whole army could live down there,'' he said.

''I think they do,'' Ichiro replied. ''I believe that, whatever Operation Snowflake is, it has its roots right here, in *chikatetsu*, with whomever controls these tunnels.''

Natsume sat back, smiling. ''Then I, perhaps, have some information that might prove useful to you,'' he said.

Ichiro stared at him. The telephone rang, and Natsume reached for it.

''Tell her I'm not here,'' Ichiro said.

Natsume picked up the phone. ''Hello,'' he said. ''Yes, Mika... No, not yet. I expect him very soon.... I will. Yes, goodbye.''

He hung up. ''Are *you* in for it,'' he said.

''What news do you have for me?'' Ichiro asked.

''I checked into those properties between the bases,'' Natsume replied. ''All of them have various owners that always turn out to be corporations owned by holding companies owned by someone else. When everything is boiled down, every piece of land, every building, every business is owned the the same man—Inazo Hashimoto."

Ichiro ran both hands through his tangled hair. "Tell me you're only joking," he said.

Natsume shook his head. "The grand old man of Japanese industrialism, one of the most beloved figures in our society, the one human being given the most credit for dragging us back to self-sufficiency after the war. Inazo Hashimoto is your quarry. Are you going to bust him, Kendo?"

"If he's guilty, yes," Ichiro replied.

Natsume laughed loudly. "Are you ever going to get it," he repeated.

"There's something else," Ichiro said.

"I know," Natsume replied. "Our boss, your dear friend, Commissioner Kawabata, is Hashi-san's nephew."

Ichiro moved slowly to his desk, sinking hard into his creaking chair. He picked up the phone and dialed his home number. Mika suddenly seemed like the lesser of several evils.

MACK BOLAN WALKED through thick fog. He felt as if he was hurrying to do something but couldn't quite remember what it was. He walked for what seemed like years. And then he heard sounds like voices and followed the sounds, their tones becoming clearer, more well-defined.

"I think he's coming around now," was the one thing that made sense to him. He became aware of his own body, of the incredible dryness of his mouth.

He woke up choking out a single word. "Water."

He opened his eyes to bright light, like the spotlights at the club he had visited. He turned his head against the glare.

"Welcome back," came Dr. Mett's damnably cordial voice.

"Water," Bolan rasped again, and someone squirted water from a plastic container into his mouth. It was enough to loosen his tongue. It was then that he became aware that he was tied to the chair upon which he was sitting.

"You are not an easy man to talk to," Mett said and nodded when Bolan was able to focus his eyes. "We added Pentothal to the tranquilizer dart I shot you with, but the best I could get from you was a string of obscenities."

"I keep my emotions locked in," Bolan said, a headache pounding hard behind his left eye. "Why didn't you just ask me if you had a question?"

"My dear man," Mett replied. "We're both men of the world. Is it necessary for us to play these games."

"You're the one who's tied *me* up, remember?"

"So I have," Mett said. "You see, I'm not quite as trusting as Hashi-san. He sees you as the Bushido warrior who has, at last, found a master. I see you as something quite else again. My men and I have decided to do Hashi-san a favor by discovering your true colors."

People were walking in and out of the light that surrounded Bolan. Sonnojoi. He was sure that Mett had brought him to the same place they had launched the attack from the night before last.

"Well, you're wrong," Bolan said.

Mett shrugged. "That is, perhaps, true. It's simply a chance I don't want to take. If I kill you right now, wrong or right, my problems are solved," he said.

"What problems are those?" Bolan asked, blinking his eyes against the pain in his head as he tried to drag himself back to full consciousness.

"My first problem," Mett began, "has to do with where your loyalty lies. My second problem is more of a . . . personal one."

"I get it," Bolan said. "You're jealous."

Mett put his hands out in front of him. "An apt word, but not exactly true. Let's just say I have invested time and money with Hashi-san, and I'd hate to lose it over a second-rate hired gun like you."

"Great," Bolan said. "He's all yours. Just untie me and I'll be on my way."

"Your choices are not quite as broad as that," Mett said and pulled a chair up in front of Bolan. He sat down and crossed his legs. "I'm going to kill you in a little while, but I'll be reasonable enough to let you die an easy death if you agree to help me."

"Help you how?"

Mett put a finger to his lips, eyes intent. "How can I put this?" he asked, thinking. "All right. You were getting awfully close to Hashi-san and would have squeezed me out first chance you had. So, to preserve my place in the scheme of things, I'll have to kill you, which will undoubtedly anger my employer, who loves you so dearly. But if I can come to him with information that would show you in a bad light, he will forget how angry he is at me and perhaps even offer me the position he had intended for you."

"The Sonnojoi work for Hashi-san?" Bolan asked.

"Yes."

"And the security force from the other night?"

"Yes. They are quite interchangeable."

"Why?"

"Honor, Mr. Bolan. The Bushido code, loyalty to the master."

"I don't understand."

Mett stood up. "It isn't my job to explain things to you. In fact, I want you to answer some questions for me."

"What about the hydrogen bombs?"

Mett sighed audibly. "He's sending them to America with the Air Force. Now it's my turn. How much of Hashi-san's operation has gone beyond you? Who else have you told?"

"You're the man who said let's stop playing games," Bolan said. "Why should I tell you anything? What's to stop me from lying to you?"

"Ah," Mett said, brightening. "I've brought you a little present that should generate some small amount of nostalgia."

He spoke in Japanese to two of the Sonnojoi who brought in a machine. "Do you recognize it?" he asked.

"It's a field telephone," Bolan said.

"I learned about these in Vietnam," Mett said. "The absolute best and quickest way to get information out of someone. I'll show you what I'm going to do."

He pulled out the two lead wires from the machine. They had been stripped, and the copper filament gleamed. He motioned for one of his men to come in and take the wires. The man stuck the exposed wires into Bolan's mouth, then clamped his jaw tightly on them.

"Now for the fun." Mett began vigorously turning an exposed crank. "These honeys can really put out the volts if you take the time to do it right."

Bolan stared at the man. He was doing it right. He'd known that field phones had been used for torturing prisoners, but he'd never seen it himself. The man continued cranking, beads of sweat popping out on his smooth face.

"That will take it out of you. Now we flip the switch. . . ."

White light exploded in Bolan's head, the incredible pain tearing him apart from the inside. He was burning with pulsing fire. Somewhere in the background he could feel that his body had stiffened and was jerking madly in the chair, but it was a pleasant, distant dream in comparison to the hell in his head, the never-ending agony.

All at once the pulsing stopped, the source of the pain was removed, leaving behind numbness and a prickliness. It was as if a thousand pins had been stuck in various places in his head and body. Someone was talking to him, but he couldn't remember or understand anything, only the pain.

His mind and body came back gradually, painfully.

"Mr. Bolan," Mett said as Bolan was finally able to understand speech. "The next one will be worse. If I kill you with this, so be it."

Bolan's eyes were blurry. He shook his head as he tried to focus on Mett. His body was still vibrating slightly. He felt totally drained of energy, his body limp and wrung out. He wanted to say something but found himself unable to talk.

"Well," Mett said, "it appears that your jaw has locked. Let me help you."

The man got up out of his chair and viciously slugged Bolan in the jaw. The Executioner crashed to the floor, chair and all.

"Set him back up," Mett said, smiling. It was the first time Bolan had ever seen him show any emotion.

Two Sonnojoi hurried into the light and set Bolan upright again. The Executioner noticed that his seizure following the last dose of electricity had loosened his bonds somewhat. And the chair itself, after being knocked around, had weakened.

Mett sat down in front of him again, grinning wide. The man was having the time of his life. "Now is that better?" he asked.

Mack Bolan thought about loyalty, the loyalty of the Bushido warrior. He had one chance and he took it. "How much are you paying these *ronin* to betray their master?" Bolan said loudly. "I'm Hashi-san's favorite. To kill me will kill him!"

"Stop!" Mett said, slapping Bolan's face repeatedly.

"Why does he silence me?" Bolan yelled. "He knows you're doing wrong. He fears the tru—"

Mett punched him, knocking him down again. Bolan's head hit the floor hard, nearly knocking him unconscious. He grimaced through the pain as Mett talked loudly in Japanese.

They set his chair upright. Bolan hoped that at least some of the Sonnojoi had understood Hashi-san's "language of business" and were translating into Japanese for the others.

Mett's face was dark and intent as he reached out and grabbed Bolan's arms. "My men know that what we are doing is the best thing for Hashi-san," he said. "Now, you will answer my questions—"

"You betray your master!" Bolan screamed.

"Damn you!" Mett rasped through clenched teeth. He grabbed the lead wires and tried to shove them back in Bolan's mouth, but the Executioner kept turning his face away.

"Traitors!" Bolan screamed. "Traitors!"

Mett finally laid the wires against Bolan's throat and hit the switch. The words froze in the Executioner's mouth as the charge slammed him back against the chair. His body vibrated in uncontrollable spasms.

He tried to hold his mind together, but white fire seared his brain, and his thoughts became oblivious as pain took over the sum total of his reality. And through it all he could smell his own charring flesh.

And then it was gone again.

He drifted back slowly, through a multitude of subsidiary shocks, and as he reassembled the scattered portions of his mind, his first conscious thought was that he wasn't going to let himself be put under the machine again—no matter what it took.

Mett was staring at him from his chair, anger replacing the good humor he had shown earlier. "Now tell me who else knows about our operation and what plans you've made."

Bolan tried to speak, but his voice was drained and powerless, a whisper the best he could manage.

Mett moved closer, and Bolan tried his bonds. They were looser, but he had no power to do anything.

"Tell me," Mett growled, leaning closer.

Bolan saw his shot and acted.

He lowered his head and came forward, chair and all. He hit Mett nose high. Numb himself, he felt nothing, but he heard both the man's nose crack loudly and Mett's muffled yell as he fell backward.

Bolan, trussed to the chair, had no balance. He fell forward, angling himself toward Mett's head as the man rolled on the floor.

Bolan twisted at the last moment, falling backward over Mett. He hit man and floor at the same time, his already creaky chair collapsing on impact. Mett groaned loudly.

Bolan rolled, kicking free of his ropes. Mett was struggling to rise. The Executioner, weak and dizzy, threw himself over Mett, going for the man's shoulder holster and coming away with an Uzi pistol.

He jammed it in Mett's throat and lay atop him, breathing heavily, trying to keep from passing out.

Sonnojoi stood all around, their shotguns pointing at him. Bolan knew he had only one card to lay on the table.

"This man has led you away from the Bushido code," he said, his voice low and hoarse. "You have dishonored yourselves and Hashi-san by your actions here today."

He looked down at Mett. The man's face was bruised and bloody, his eyes dead things through which nothing good could ever be seen. He stared at Bolan with an empty, useless soul.

Bolan pulled the trigger under the man's chin, the pop muffled in the folds of flesh around his neck. Mett jerked once, blood gushing from his mouth and ears, then fell back, his eyes looking just the same as they had when he'd been alive.

Bolan rose shakily, nearly falling twice. The Sonnojoi still faced him, their weapons ready. The Executioner turned a circle, staggering.

"It was right that he should die," Bolan said to the warriors.

There was deadly silence for nearly a minute, then one by one, two dozen Sonnojoi turned their shotguns toward themselves and pulled the triggers. Twenty-four men, bound by an honor they didn't really understand—an honor established by forty-seven *ronin*—took their own lives in the warehouse rather than face the humiliation they had brought upon the name of Inazo Hashimoto.

Bolan made an effort to leave, but his body wouldn't listen. He sat, for just a minute, next to the body of Dr. Mett. And then he slept.

14

Mika Ichiro stepped precariously over the knees of one of the members of the Special Services squad as she tried to bring tea to the men jammed into her small home. Both she and Kendo were proud of their house. It was the result of many years of savings from the meager policeman's salary Kendo received, in addition to the money she made teaching the art of origami to primary-school students.

All the furniture and every bit of floor space in the living room and dining room were filled with men dressed in dark olive drab with blackened faces. Their weapons rested upon their knees or in hip holsters. Mika was afraid of guns, but she was a cop's wife and accepted all that it meant with dignity and quiet reticence. Her husband was there with her, and that was all that mattered.

Lieutenant Kendo Ichiro turned on the motor of the slide projector as soon as Mika had served tea. It was just getting dark outside. They didn't have much time.

"Would you please turn off the house lights?" he asked his wife as she moved through the group of men, back to the kitchen.

"Hai," she said, lowering her head in the customary subservient manner.

When the lights went out, Ichiro turned on the projector bulb, and an unfocused picture blurred his white wall. Before he adjusted the focus, he addressed the men seated before him.

"There is a reason why we are meeting here in my home, in secrecy," he said. "All your careers will be put in jeopardy by what you are taking part in. I am about to tell you about a mission in which we will be acting illegally, without sanction from anyone higher than me. The mission will be dangerous, and I can't guarantee what will happen to you after it is over—*if* you survive. Anyone who wants to may leave now. No one will think the worse of you. I ask only that you say nothing about it until tomorrow, at which time all truth will be known."

Ichiro waited. He looked down at Natsume, who sat on the floor beside him. The man smiled easily. No one got up to leave, and Ichiro breathed a sigh of relief.

He reached out and focused the picture on the wall. It was one of the pictures of the underground hangars that he had lifted from the history book that afternoon.

"Chikatetsu," he said, pointing to the picture. It showed Japanese Zeroes lined up in neat military rows. "I have reason to believe that a private army of Sonnojoi lives underground, here, in the old tunnels between Yokota and Tachikowa Air Bases. I believe

they are responsible for a large cocaine trade, plus I believe they are the ones who kidnapped Dr. Lawrence Norwood and were responsible for his death. I also think that a man whose name you might be familiar with is the head of this organization—Inazo Hashimoto.''

He heard the murmurs that ran through the room, but they died quickly. He threw another picture up on the wall, this one a blueprint of the underground complex.

''I believe a large cocaine shipment, bound for the United Sates, is going to change hands tonight. I intend to stop it. It is unlikely that I could get a warrant because of the political control exercised by Mr. Hashimoto, so I'm taking it upon myself to go in and stop the operation.''

There was general agreement around the room.

He threw up another picture, this one showing a blueprint of the complex from ground level. ''Here is a ground view of *chikatetsu*. The small notches you see at ground level were originally designed as air passages to the outside. Now look at this.''

He put on another slide of the same thing, only this time there was a superimposition of buildings on the ground. ''As you can see, five buildings were placed over the air passages, all of them owned by Hashimoto. Of the five, four of them are operating businesses. The fifth, though, here—'' he pointed to the picture ''—is an old storage warehouse. I believe that these air passages are used as entries to the underground. We're going to try the warehouse and see what we can find. Are there any questions?''

A voice came from the darkness. "There are twenty-five of us. How large is the force of the Sonnojoi?''

"I have no idea," Ichiro said, "no idea at all.''

BOLAN SAT in the house of death, breathing in its smell, and collected his strength. Light was fading beyond the high warehouse windows. He'd been sleeping for several hours. He looked at his watch, but the face was charred and broken. Every muscle in his body was sore and aching as he turned to look at the body of Dr. Mett.

He reached over and looked at Mett's watch. Nearly seven. He had another hour, two at the most. He stood slowly, painfully, and looked around for his guns. Bolan saw the field telephone, and anger coursed through him. Bending, he grabbed the machine and threw it viciously at the cement floor. It shattered on impact. The feeling was better than the fix he got from ten cups of coffee. The torture box brought him back to reality. He had to hurry.

Mett's car, a Honda sedan, sat parked near the warehouse doors. Bolan hurried toward it. The keys were in the ignition, and his combat harness lay on the floorboards of the passenger's side.

Bolan slipped into the harness while trying to put things together in his mind. The deal was going down tonight. Hashi-san's steel mill was about five miles from Yokota, and he was halfway between the two places. The base was sealed, but the mill probably wasn't. He could be at the Asano Corporation in a few minutes. It seemed the logical place to start.

The Executioner kicked the accelerator and jammed the car into gear, backing out with a squeal of tires. The sky was clear, no sign of rain. He moved out into the twilight. It struck him as odd that so little development had gone on in an area so heavily populated.

Traffic was thick as rush-hour motorists made their way out to the suburbs from Tokyo proper. As he tried to maneuver his way through it, he thought about the two hydrogen bombs set to make their way to the United States. The logical choices to drop off the bombs would be Travis Air Base in California or Andrews on the East Coast. Both were near major population centers. If Hashi-san wanted to regain his family honor, he could do away with millions of innocent people in the first blast of Dr. Norwood's toys.

As he neared the entrance to the Asano Corporation, a great many connections began to make sense. The cocaine was a front for the bombs. Of course Jamison didn't know he'd be toting nuclear death. Hank Jamison was just a cheap hood looking to get rich, his own kind of retaliation against the Air Force, which he blamed for his problems. Operation Snowflake was an elaborate scheme designed by Hashi-san to settle an oath he'd made in 1945 when he adopted the code of the Bushido. Human life, including the life of his daughter, meant nothing to the old man.

Bolan left the main drag, moving down the private road that led to the steel mill. The huge wrought-iron gates were closed and barred, although the parking lot within the structure was filled with cars. Above the entrance was the kanji script he had seen on the helicopter. A glowing red sun was painted between the characters.

He hit the horn, waiting to see what came to greet him. Nothing. He beeped again, but nothing happened. He climbed out of the car and moved to look through the slats of the gate. Moving back several paces, he got a running start and jumped, catching the bars and climbing the rest of the fifteen-foot height.

Bolan moved quickly through the parking lot that fronted railroad lines and a long row of towering blast furnaces where the pig iron was melted and transported in ladles to the hearth furnaces. He found a door leading right into the mill. A blast of heat greeted him as he entered. So far, he'd seen no one.

The Executioner picked up his pace, looking for Hashi-san's office. He ran down a short hallway that opened onto the main floor of the factory which was the size of two football fields. Conveyor belts ran the length of the building, along with overhead trams that carried the ladles to the now dormant hearth furnaces where the pig iron was superheated with steel and flux to make a ribbon of workable steel.

Everything was shut down, although it was still extremely hot. The whole plant was empty, and Bolan began to suspect that Hashi-san controlled every aspect of his warrior's lives as employer and benefactor. But where were they?

He moved quickly through the plant, coming out finally at an administrative section that was separated from the rest of the building by two sets of double doors. Bolan entered, walking past empty offices. The hallway finally ended at a door marked in English Mr. Hashimoto.

The door was locked. Bolan kicked it in and found himself in a receptionist's area. The door beyond that was marked Private. The Executioner entered.

He was standing in a large office that could have belonged to an ancient shogun. The low desk sat on the floor with a cushion behind it. In front of the desk were many cushions, for whomever had an audience with the great man. Instead of carpeting, a straw mat covered the floor. The walls were hung with swords and tapestry depictions of ancient *ronin*. Three-foot high incense sticks burned thickly on a portable Buddhist temple in the corner. It was a study in simple elegance, a traditional Japanese room. And it didn't help the Executioner one bit.

He wasn't sure what he'd been looking for, but it obviously wasn't here. He turned to leave, then thought of all the cars in the parking lot. Those people had to be somewhere. He thought about sumo wrestling and the Aussie's theory, then moved back through the office, going to the walls themselves.

He began pulling down tapestries to bare the walls, then stopped before a cloth painting depicting Asano himself, as a ghost, and the suicide of the forty-seven *ronin*. His hand was shaking as he reached out and pulled it from the wall. Behind it was an elevator door containing only one button—down. *"Chikatetsu,"* Bolan whispered and reached for the button.

HASHI-SAN WATCHED as the huge ball was lowered into the box marked Radar Bay by the small, one-man crane they used upstairs for loading pig iron. As soon as it was gently settled in its mooring, several of his men climbed up the box and began stuffing one-pound packages of cocaine around it. This was the bomb destined for Travis Air Base in California. This one would be for Hiroshima. It promised to kill a great many more people than that original bomb had. Payment, plus interest.

He was most satisfied. Honor would soon be partially served through the greed of the American airmen.

Junko sat beside him, in the driver's seat of the golf cart. She seemed deep in thought, unhappy somehow, although he couldn't understand what could possibly bother her at the hour of his greatest triumph. Around him stretched his kingdom, the *chikatetsu*, hewn from rock and earth by his ancestors, completed with steel and concrete by his warriors. Hundreds of his followers worked quickly, all wanting to take part in this final realization of a long-held dream. His men were devoted to him, as their fathers had been. He'd brought them into the factory at an early age, had taken care of them morally and financially, and they repaid him with undying devotion. He was their master, and they lived for his service.

"Where's Mett?" Junko asked. "The Americans will soon come to take their packages."

"We do not need him at this stage," Hashi-san said. "In fact, I've been thinking that with the addition of Mr. Bolan as our retainer, we may not need Dr. Mett at all anymore."

"I'm not so sure that he'll be interested in joining you, Father," she said, staring down at the steering wheel.

"Nonsense!" Hashi-san said, as always ignoring anything he didn't want to hear. "He is an honorable man and seeks the company of others as honorable as himself."

"It is his country you are preparing to attack."

"What's a country? Men serve other men. A country is just the ground men live upon. It means nothing to the warrior."

"But, Father—"

"Enough! I've spoken."

The fitting of the bomb had been completed in the first box. Next came the delicate part. The lid was lowered slowly to the box. A small line with an attached hook dangled from its center. As the top came down, the hook was attached to a small ring that protruded through the camouflage curtain of cocaine. Then the lid was nailed on and the cord tightened. When the box was opened, the cord would pull against the ring, setting off the synchronized charges within the bomb itself. The end result would be a glorious release of the energy within the plutonium atom, a power equal to the sun itself.

"Goodbye, California," Hashi-san said happily as the box was nailed tightly and loaded by forklift into the back of the waiting truck that Captain Jamison had left with them.

A telephone rang across the span of the empty hangar, and one of his men ran to get it. He approached Hashi-san hurriedly a minute later.

"My Hashi-san," he began, bowing low, "two visitors are within the underground and moving this way."

"Yes?" the man inquired.

"Your nephew, Commissioner Kawabata, is coming by cart right now on urgent business," the man said. "The other is Bolan-san. He entered at the mill and has been walking this way."

Junko looked up, her eyes hurt and fearful. "Bolan—" she began, but her father stopped her.

"Don't worry," he said. "I would have preferred to break the news of all this to Bolan-san in my own way, but since that is denied me, I'll talk to him now."

Junko looked at him, but the rock hardness of his eyes kept her from saying any more.

"Here comes your nephew now," the Sonnojoi said, and immediately they could hear the hum of his cart's electric motor.

Hashi-san looked toward the tunnel, watching the glowing eyes of the cart boring into him as it closed the distance between them. It was a peaceful, quiet world he had in *chikatetsu*, a world where the ancient and the modern could be contemplated at leisure.

The cart pulled up next to him, and he could tell immediately that his nephew was upset. He'd always been high-strung as a boy.

"Uncle," Kawabata said, bowing his head before Hashi-san.

"What is it, Shusaku?"

Kawabata looked up at the man, shaking his head. "Hashi-san, I fear that one of my detectives has discovered what goes on here," he said. "A man named Ichiro."

"Yes, I've heard of him."

"He's been tracking down the man they call the Executioner, the one I had released from jail for you." Kawabata looked behind him, as if fearful something would spring upon him from behind.

"I've been trying to keep watch on him, Uncle," the commissioner continued. "One of my men at his station house found history books on his desk, one of them opened to a section about *chikatetsu*. And now I can't find him anywhere. All the elite of Ichiro's Special Services unit are missing, too. I fear the lieutenant plans to raid this installation."

"Without a warrant?" Hashi-san asked, his eyes dancing.

"This is serious, Uncle," Kawabata said. "My name is on those prison transfer forms. If they connect me..."

"You always were a selfish boy," Hashi-san replied. "Who put you through school, selfish boy?"

"You, Uncle."

"Who found you a rich wife? Who handed you the position you now hold? Who covers up your disgusting sexual indiscretions?"

"You, Uncle, you."

"Well, now you will do something for me, Shusaku," the old man said. "I now seek repayment for all I've done in the past. If the security of *chikatetsu* is to be breached by your men, then certainly you will be able to send them away."

"I don't know if—"

"You don't understand, Nephew." Hashi-san fixed him with cold eyes. "You have no choice. I can take away your rich wife and powerful position. I can take your clothes and your life. You *will* do as I ask, Shusaku. There are no alternatives."

"Yes, Hashi-san," the man said with downcast eyes, a victim of his own weakness.

Hashi-san nodded. "Stay here," he said. "Wait. I have a meeting with a real man, something you wouldn't understand." He nodded to Junko. "Let's go."

THE ELEVATOR OPENED into another world.

Mack Bolan, the Executioner, walked out of the

small lift and into a land of old dreams. The underground was huge and wide open. To his right was a wide hangar full of ancient fighter planes. To his left an open corridor stretched far into the distance.

He recognized the planes, called Zeroes. They had been the best airplane in the skies in the early days of the Second World War and had nearly destroyed the entire American fleet at Pearl Harbor. He also recognized the red circle painted on their sides—the Rising Sun of Japanese imperialism. They had been sitting in the hangar, untouched, for over forty years. He saw hundreds of planes lined four abreast, reaching for a distant wall. But the corridor extended far beyond the wall. The immensity of this complex was impressive. The area was meticulously clean, and evenly spaced spotlights illuminated the area at regular intervals. Beams of steel crisscrossed the structure for reinforcement and he could hear the motors of monstrous fans bringing fresh air into this tomb of the past.

And hanging from the beams, every twenty feet, large banners bearing Hashi-san's likeness fluttered in the machine-generated air. On the banners he was dressed as his ancestor Asano in ancient warrior garb with a samurai sword. The man had built an entire empire devoted to praising himself and covering up his own guilt. A mind so clever, spent fooling itself.

Bolan drew Big Thunder and began walking. He hadn't gone ten feet before noticing something that wasn't forty years old—a small TV camera tracking his movements. They knew he was here. Fine. The Executioner didn't have time for stealth, anyway.

He walked quickly, moving past row upon row of ancient airplanes, his boot heels echoing on the cement floor. After several minutes he passed the hangar wall and came upon double thick cinder block that housed weapons, ammo and drums of gasoline.

The antique weapons were set neatly in racks, including the single-shot Meiji carbines that had even been dated in 1945. The ammo he ignored completely. It would have broken down and lost its potency long ago. But the gasoline had possibilities.

He passed the weapons racks and moved to the barrels. There were a couple of hundred, stacked about thirty feet high. A great deal would have been lost to evaporation, but if the barrels had been sealed properly, there would still be kick left in some of them. Underground, the temperature was the same year round, perfect storage conditions.

He tapped a barrel with Big Thunder. It rang partly full. Filing the information in his mind, he hurried on.

After he passed the dump, he came to a motor pool full of three-wheeled electric carts. These had to be Hashi-san's. There was also a large ramp that sloped from the middle of the building at a thirty-five-degree angle to the ceiling. This had to be where the Sonnojoi entered. He took a cart and proceeded, television cameras recording his movements the whole time.

After the motor pool he passed a barracks area where bunks were tiered three high on poles spaced at regular intervals. Hundreds of men could sleep here, and Bolan began to get the feeling of a unit. He drove on, past yet another section of planes.

Bolan saw the lights approaching as he cleared the next section of Zeroes. It was only one cart, and he knew it was coming in response to the TV cameras. Hashi-san knew better than to send a few men to take him. He wasn't surprised, then, to find himself confronted by the Bushido master himself. Unfortunately, Junko was with him.

She pulled the cart to within ten feet of Bolan and stopped. The two stared at one another across the space of hangar. Bolan's mouth was dry.

"I'm glad you've come, Bolan-san," Hashimoto said, standing in the cart. "I would have brought you here soon myself, anyway. Now you can share my greatest triumph."

"You amaze me," Bolan said. "How could you expect me to share the deaths of innocents with you?"

The man's eyes narrowed. "You don't understand. I want you to share the fulfillment of my honor!"

"Honor more important than the lives of my own people?"

"Yes!" Hashi-san said, amazed. "Of course. *I* am your people, Mack Bolan. You are the warrior. I am your master. We share the code."

"You've used me from the first," Bolan said, his eyes drifting to Junko's. Hers were wet with tears. "At the pachinko parlor, how did you know?"

"My man at the American Embassy." Hashimoto shrugged. "I still didn't know where Norwood was hiding, but I was able to keep tabs on the old man through the embassy. When I couldn't kill you there, I found out about you. I determined then that you were the person to succeed me, to carry on the dynasty that I've made."

"The attack on the highway..."

"A test," Hashi-san said. "To be sure."

"Had you been wrong, Junko would have been killed."

"But she wasn't."

"What about the cocaine, the...poison you hate so much?"

"Like a vaccine, Bolan-san, I used an amount of the poison to cure it. Once I have fulfilled my honor against the people of America, I will eradicate the poison in my country. I now have deep contacts within the Yakuza on all levels of their drug operation. From here, with your help, I can finish them."

Bolan stared at him. "And you've used me to kill your Air Force connections, too."

"Many streams branch from a single river, my son," Hashi-san said. "I helped to pit you against them to still too many mouths who had too much to say. It's a game, and the priorities continue to change. Where is Dr. Mett?"

"Dead," Bolan said.

"You see? You have done me another favor."

"And Junko, what about her?"

Hashi-san smiled. "A happy accident," he said. "The human heart controls itself. I couldn't have planned her love for you had I set out to do it."

Junko had buried her face in her hands and cried softly. And once again Bolan realized how wrong it was to let someone become close to him.

"I'm going to kill you, you know," he said to the man, and Hashimoto grimaced at the words.

"You can't," he said. "I've brought my empire to this moment for you. Immortality is continuance."

"I deal in mortality," Bolan said. "Nothing more."

Hashi-san's face hardened then, and Bolan could tell he was readjusting his priorities, just as the Executioner had done many times in the past several days. "If that is the case, Bolan-san," he began, "then I will leave you with a far more difficult choice than you have anticipated. The Executioner will have to prove his own honor. Junko! Get out of the cart!"

The woman looked at her father with pleading eyes. "Get out!" he ordered.

She got out of the cart, reaching beside the seat for the MAC-10 she had used at the nightclub. She stared vacantly at Bolan, her face stained with tears.

"Either bring him with us or kill him," Hashi-san said as he jumped into the driver's seat.

Bolan raised Big Thunder, but Junko put herself between the two men, the gun still held at her side. The old man threw his cart into reverse, backing away, using his daughter as a shield.

"I'm going after him," Bolan said, his foot stepping down on the gas.

"If you do," she returned, "you'll be dead before you get past me."

He stared at her, and emotions threatened to tear them both apart. "He could kill millions," Bolan said. "Innocent people, children. You can't let that happen."

"He is my father," she said through trembling lips. "I honor his n-name ... and the code of the Bushido that is his life."

"You could kill me?"

The tears ran down her face. "I love you, Mack Bolan," she said. "But my blood...is his blood. Will you not join us?"

Mack swallowed hard. "I've got to go after him, and I don't have any more time."

She primed the stuttergun. "To pass, you will have to kill me ... or I will kill you."

"I ... can't kill you," he said. "My God, Junko, I—"

"Then you will die at my hand."

She raised her weapon. Bolan's muscles tensed involuntarily as the MAC-10 traced a line on him. "Just turn around," he pleaded, "walk away. For God's sake ... please!"

She was shaking, "Honor," she said, then screamed it. "Honor!"

He saw the look then, the same one he'd seen on the highway and in the nightclub, and he knew that she would kill him.

He dove from the cart just as she fired, tearing up the seat and steering wheel. His own instinct kicked in, he rolled and came up firing on automatic.

The bullets caught her chest and picked her up off the ground and threw her backward. She went down hard on the concrete, arms and legs twisted like a rag doll thrown in the corner.

Bolan ran to her, tears blinding his own eyes. Her chest was a pool of blood, and her limbs twitched. A trickle of red ran from the corners of her mouth. Her eyes were wide and fearful as she looked up at him.

The woman who had given him so much lay dying by his own hand. And for what? Honor? If this was honor, Bolan wanted no part of it.

Junko tried to speak, but she could only utter a deep, painful gurgle. Bolan couldn't stand it anymore. Bringing up Big Thunder, he put a bullet through her brain to end the agony.

And he wished it had been his own brain he'd put the bullet in. Junko now had peace.

15

Hashimoto drove back to the meeting place, his thoughts on Mack Bolan. With Mett dead and Bolan a traitor, he'd have to begin training a new successor. His men had assembled in this cleared hangar space and stood in full dress, including the helmets, for this historic occasion.

He drove in front of the ranks who stood, in formation and at attention, awaiting him. The lid of the second bomb crate was being nailed into place, and his nephew stood studying the large wooden box.

He climbed down from the cart and walked up and down the lines of men with his hands behind his back. "Faithful retainers!" he called. "You have been with me for many years, most of you coming into my service from childhood. I have always been a good and kind father to you, and you, in return, have showered me with trust and devotion.

"Now we stand at the brink of a miracle, ancient codes of vengeance wrought with modern fire. This is a glorious day for the name of Asano, a glorious day for all of us! Rejoice!"

The men cheered with fervor, reveling in the completion of a long-held dream. Their cheering echoed like the rumble of thunder through the cavern. Hashi-san put up his hands for silence.

"And once we have accomplished the fulfillment of these dreams, we may begin the work of driving the foreign invaders from our lands for all time. To the Sonnojoi!"

More shouting as the men in black helmets thrust their fists high in the air. Hashi-san turned to see an Air Force jeep drive up from the Yokota end of the tunnel. Jamison and O'Brian climbed out with two suitcases.

The old man walked over to them to shake hands.

"What's all the excitement, Chief?" Jamison asked.

"We are simply glad to complete our bargain, Captain," Hashi-san said with a catlike smile and a cold demeanor. "If you'll wait a moment, we'll load the other crate onto your truck."

"Don't you want to count the money first?" Jamison asked.

"The money?" he said, then looked at the suitcases. "Ah, just so. We are all honorable men, Captain. I will trust that the amount is correct."

Jamison bowed. "And I will trust that the goods are all accounted for."

"All packaged up for you, as I promised," Hashi-san said and hoped sincerely that it would be Jamison himself who'd pry the lid off the nuclear device.

A Sonnojoi manning the phone ran up and whispered in Hashimoto's ear. "A small force has made its way into the complex," he whispered, lifting the visor on his helmet to speak. "Two dozen, no more. They move in this direction."

Hashi-san nodded. "Ah, so, so, so."

"Problems?" O'Brian asked.

"Small ones, Sergeant," Hashi-san said, bowing. "It will delay your loading for just a minute or two longer." He waved his arm to get Kawabata's attention, then walked over to talk to his nephew.

"They're here, aren't they?" Kawabata asked nervously.

"Yes, Shusaku. They are here. You must act like a man today. I hope you're up to the task."

"But . . ."

He waved the man off. "Take the cart. Hurry. My men will be right behind you."

Reluctantly Kawabata jumped into the cart and started off, Hashi-san giving the order for the rest of his men to hurry after on foot.

They went without a word, nearly two hundred men moving silently into the solitude of the cavern. Hashi-san turned from them and addressed Jamison.

"I've never ridden in an airplane before," Hashimoto said. "Tell me what it's like, Captain."

BOLAN DROVE THE CART quickly through the cavern. He moved without thought, his insides deadened, only the strength of his mission pulling him forward. He drove in a haze as alternating sections of planes, ammo and housing whirled dizzily past him. His sense of honor was charred. It was his duty that spurred him—and his hatred of Hashi-san. It was personal now, as personal as it could be.

Somewhere off in the fog of reality that clouded his brain, he heard a sound, a snap. Then all at once he was out of control as the cart veered wildly.

It flipped over just as Bolan jumped to safety. He hit the floor hard and rolled. Ingrained habit lessened the impact, and Bolan looked up in time to watch the cart roll over and over, finally resting upside down and skidding loudly into the wheel struts of a Zero. The plane buckled slowly, angling down upon the dead cart like a bird on a nest.

"Mack Bolan," he heard a familiar voice say. "You're under arrest."

He sat up, turning to see Lieutenant Ichiro and his small squad standing before him. Ichiro held a silenced .38, smoke curling from the barrel. The man had shot his tire out.

"Put your hands behind your head," Ichiro demanded as Bolan climbed to his feet.

"There's no time for this," Bolan said. "Hashimoto is about to load two hydrogen bombs on an airplane bound for the States. If we don't stop him..."

"Why should I believe you?" Ichiro asked.

Bolan looked at him. "I've just killed the woman who was very important to me," he said. "I'm trying to save the lives of millions. Come with me if you want, but don't try and stop me."

With that he began walking away from them.

"Stop!" Ichiro called, but Bolan ignored him. Hashimoto was all that mattered.

The lieutenant ran to catch up with him. "You don't give an inch, do you?" he asked.

"Neither do you," Bolan said, "or you wouldn't be down here. We just need to cut through the crap and get on with it."

"All right," Ichiro said, waving for his men to follow. "What are we up against?"

"No telling," Bolan replied. "A small army, perhaps. The bombs. The U.S. Air Force and—" he gestured around "—any number of surprises."

The first surprise was not long in coming. A lone cart approached them from the endless distance. It stopped thirty feet from them, and a single figure Bolan didn't recognize got out and walked up to stand ten feet from them.

"Commissioner Kawabata," Ichiro whispered, and nothing surprised Bolan anymore. He just shook his head.

"You are trespassing," Kawabata said. "This is private property, and you have no authority to be here."

"I've taken it upon myself," Ichiro began, "to investigate—"

"You are hereby removed from all duties, Lieutenant. You must return to the surface immediately. You are in violation of the law."

"No!" Ichiro said. "We will continue our investigation."

"Don't be an idiot," the commissioner said. "There is a large force behind me, and they would be well within their rights to fire on trespassers. You would all be killed. There's nothing here you need worry about."

Bolan drew Big Thunder. There was absolutely no time to deal with Hashi-san's errand boy.

"You are all Japanese," Kawabata continued. "Hashi-san is a father to you, to all of—"

Bolan fired once, the slug ripping a third eye in the man's forehead. He fell silently, his head cracking loudly on the concrete floor.

The Executioner turned to the assembled men, who looked at him uneasily. "We need to work fast to give ourselves an edge. Forget this man. He's nothing now. Let's go!"

He and Ichiro shared a look, the police officer nodding with tight lips. "Come on!" Ichiro shouted.

They were right at the dividing edge that separated hanger from ammo dump. Bolan split his small force in half. Twelve men began pulling out gasoline barrels and rolling them to the open corridor. The other twelve pulled the blocks out from under the aircraft wheels and pushed the planes by the tail out of formation and into the open passage.

Bolan hurried the operation as shadows from the charging Sonnojoi flickered far down the passage. He moved to the men with the barrels. They had formed a chain, pulling barrels of gas out and rolling them hand-to-hand to stack in the passage. The Executioner took hold of one of the barrels and rolled it in the direction of the oncoming attack force.

On the flat, level plane of the cavern, the barrel rolled straight and true, moving maybe a hundred yards before finally running out of steam and creaking to a stop.

"Roll the others!" Bolan called. "Keep going till we run out of time!"

He ran back to the planes where Ichiro was setting them out in a straight line, back to front. "We've only got a few minutes," he said. "What we need is a man in the cockpit with an automatic and ammo, and two to push the plane. We can squeeze nine planes that way. Put me in the lead plane."

"Got it." Ichiro began issuing orders.

Bolan climbed onto the wing of the first Zero. The body of the plane was squat, the canopy totally glass. It unlatched, then slid back, leaving a windshield in front. The red circle on the fuselage glowed hotly. It could have represented the ball of fire from a nuclear blast.

From his vantage point he could see them coming, jogging at forced march pace. They were nearing the field of barrels, which was growing by the second.

Bolan slid back the canopy and hoisted himself into the plane, kicking out the front windshield.

He stood on the small seat and looked behind. Others were climbing into the cockpits, including Ichiro with his M-16 and extra clips. This may not have been the ultimate in situation ethics, but Bolan had nothing else to work with. He could have fought a holding action successfully, but it was progress he need to make right now.

"Form a line, prone!" he called to the men still on the floor. "When I give the word, fire on the barrels!"

As his men rushed to comply, Bolan could see the Sonnojoi entering his impromptu mine field. He fought down the urge to fire immediately and bided his time, watching them move closer.

"Fire!" he yelled when they were twenty yards away, and M-16s rattled below him. There was an endless second of waiting, then the first barrel went up.

The whole tunnel shook as orange fire exploded sequentially down the long corridor like a monstrous string of firecrackers. The force nearly knocked Bolan out of the plane as men on the ground fell and loose rock dropped from the ceiling. The floor cracked beneath them.

Down the tunnel Sonnojoi screamed. Human torches ran in circles with nowhere to go. Those who escaped the blasts began returning fire as the thickening black smoke roiled through the caverns. The overworked exhaust system was no match for so much smoke.

"Let's go! Let's go! Let's go!" Bolan screamed, and his men ran to take positions behind the aircraft.

His Zero rolled quickly into the kill zone. He had the high ground and began firing down on those left alive as his plane slid into the battlefield of burning men and choking smoke.

Shotguns kicked back at him, taking out chunks of the sheet-metal body of the plane. Bolan screamed out his own heartrending frustration on man after man as he cleared a path for those behind. The stench of burning flesh was overpowering.

Sonnojoi below were tearing off their helmets as oily smoke got beneath the visors, blinding them. Bolan was losing it, too. He looked down in the cockpit and found goggles to put on.

He emptied a clip from Big Thunder and jammed in another. He looked behind at grounded Zeroes—ghost planes moving through the fog of smoke—that left a trail of bodies in their wake.

His plane suddenly veered to the right when one of his men crumpled to the ground with a belly hit. The other tried to keep pushing, but three Sonnojoi jumped him, knocking him to the ground before blowing his head off, point-blank, with a shotgun.

The plane spun, then stopped, and Bolan jumped out of the cockpit as Sonnojoi swarmed the wings. He blasted three in a line before Ichiro's plane pulled up beside him. The cop added his gun to Bolan's.

"Come on!" Ichiro yelled, and Bolan jumped to the wing of the man's plane, firing behind him to protect the men pushing the thing.

They reached the end of the burning gas field and turned to catch the Sonnojoi in cross fire. The other planes had stopped moving, bogged down in the bodies that littered the floor. The men were now engaged in hand-to-hand combat.

Bolan saw Ichiro's assistant Natsume, grab his throat, and blood welled between his fingers as he fell forward, bouncing off the wing to roll onto the burning ground. Ichiro screamed out the man's name, then jammed another clip into his M-16, methodically shooting one punk after another in the head.

And all at once the Sonnojoi crumpled, their spirit broken. They ran, in full retreat, back down the hall toward the steel mill.

"I'm going for Hashimoto!" Bolan yelled and jumped off the wing to run the corridor, heedless of Ichiro's shouts behind him.

He moved, the tension in his body driving him hard, pushing him beyond his limits. Bolan felt nothing, neither pain nor fatigue. It was as if he were outside of his body, viewing it from a distance.

Within minutes he could see the Air Force truck in the distance, O'Brian trying unsuccessfully to operate the forklift that would load his last crate into the back of the vehicle. Thick clouds of smoke rolled into the chamber with the Executioner.

As he closed on them, they abandoned the crate and jumped into the truck, leaving Hashi-san alone to face the Executioner.

The old man waited calmly, standing by his crate of death until Bolan, breathing hard, reached him.

"You are quite a man, Bolan-san," Hashimoto said. "I must assume that my daughter is dead?"

"Assume only that *you're* dead, you bastard," Bolan said in a low voice.

"I really fail to understand you," Hashi-san said, backing up against the crate. "We are two men of honor, operating beyond the normal constraints of society."

"I'm protecting society," Bolan said. "That's what you never understood."

"My dear man," Hashi-san replied, "I fail to see the difference in us. We both have a quest. We both . . . kill when it's necessary."

"I don't kill innocent people," Bolan replied and unholstered his AutoMag.

"Of course you do." Hashimoto laughed. "It's unavoidable. Wars do that."

Bolan turned a thumb to himself. "Not this war!" he yelled, the anger nearly overpowering. "Not *my* war. My war is against people like you. My war is fought so that innocents aren't trampled under the boots of people who think they can use flesh and blood any way they want to satisfy their own selfishness."

"But, Bolan—"

"Shut up! You can talk all night and play all the word games you want to compare us, but we're in no way alike. Don't you understand? All this, all this pain and suffering you've caused is so you won't have to admit to yourself what a coward you are!"

The rock cracked then, Hashi-san's face sagging, his lips sputtering. He was an old, frightened man, desperately trying to keep from admitting the lie his life had been.

Bolan took a step closer. He could smell the fear rolling off the old man in waves. "They've existed like you from the dawn of time," Bolan said. "Butchers who've killed and tortured and raped and degraded, all in the name of something high and mighty that isn't real—Hitler, Stalin—join the ranks. They don't come any worse than you. I'm going to enjoy killing you. God help me, I'm going to enjoy it."

A single shot rang through the cavern.

16

Bolan sped through the remaining two miles of the tunnel, driving the Air Force jeep as fast as it would go. The surface was flat and level at first, then he hit a gentle upgrade as the entire tunnel ran upward toward ground level. He lost the floodlights then and had to drive in darkness.

Headlights on, he saw nothing but black ahead. The truck had come this way, so Bolan knew that it must lead to an exit. He goosed the accelerator and hoped for the best.

Bolan suddenly crested a hill and found himself skidding across level ground. He regained control as he drove through an empty hangar. The hundred-foot doors were pushed open to reveal the flight line in the distance. It was lit by nighttime runway lights.

A KC-135 Stratolifter sat on the line, the whole tail end of the plane hinged down to ground level as a crate marked Radar Bay was loaded into it. Mack Bolan set his jaw and drove toward it.

"COME ON!" Jamison screamed from inside the massive cargo compartment as the forklift driver tried to maneuver the heavy crate up the back ramp and into the bay of the huge machine.

O'Brian stood beside him scanning the night as the forklift bumped up the ramp and slowly set the load down ten feet inside the cargo bay. Crates and equipment of all sizes stretched a hundred feet toward the cockpit.

"Get out of here!" Jamison yelled as soon as the airman had set down the load. "Quick!"

"What's the rush, Captain?"

"Get out!" Jamison screamed, drawing his .45 and aiming it at the man, who got the message and put the electric truck into reverse.

"Oh, shit," O'Brian whispered, pointing into the night. "Here he comes."

Jamison saw the headlights moving closer. He grabbed the intercom mike from the loading instrument bay and called his pilot. "Waverly," he said. "Take it out now."

"What are you talking about, Hank?" the voice returned. "The bay's still open!"

"Take it out now!" Jamison yelled. "I've got bay control on manual. I'll put it up!"

"We're not tied down yet," one of his men called from deeper in the cargo hold.

"Screw it!"

The jeep had bumped up on the runway and was closing on them fast.

"We don't even have clearance," the pilot called. "Hank—"

"Listen, you son of a bitch," Jamison said. "Go now, or I'll come up there and blow your goddamned head off!"

"Roger."

Engines already revved, the huge bird started down the runway, jerking the forklift off the side of the ramp. The operator screamed as the weight of his machine came down atop him. Sparks flew where the ramp dragged the runway. O'Brian watched as the jeep almost caught them.

"What do we do?" O'Brian yelled into the rushing wind.

"He's your problem," Jamison said. "You handle him!"

With that he shoved O'Brian out the back of the plane and reached for the ramp door control.

BOLAN WATCHED as a man came flying out of the back of the plane to land hard on his hood. The Executioner veered, and O'Brian scrabbled for the windshield, trying to grab hold of something.

Big Thunder lay on the passenger's seat. The Executioner picked it up and fired through the windshield. O'Brian's guts exploded. The sergeant lost his grip and slipped from the jeep, bouncing once on the runway before lying still.

Bolan jammed the gas pedal down as the plane picked up speed, and then he heard the hum of the motor that raised the ramp flush against the plane. The sparks stopped as the door began to lift, and Bolan pushed for the last ounce of go in the jeep. His front wheels bumped up onto the ramp.

Half of the jeep was on the ramp before its back wheels were lifted off the ground. The passenger's side window blew out, and Bolan caught a glimpse of Jamison firing at him before the captain disappeared behind some equipment.

The ramp was closing, and the jeep balanced on its end. Bolan stood up in the seat and climbed over the broken windshield. He ran down the hood and dove for the inside of the plane, hitting hard and rolling to a stop beside the crate containing the bomb.

Seconds later the jeep rolled down the ramp toward the inside of the jumbo jet, wedging itself into the gap between the ramp and the plane. The ramp stalled, halfway open, with a horrible grinding noise.

Bolan ejected the clip from Big Thunder and planted another. The plane was building up speed. O'Brian's body was a distant dot on the landscape. There was a radio somewhere near him because Bolan could hear the pilot frantically calling.

"Jamison! The damned ramp's not closed yet! We're going too fast to stop now.... I don't know if I can . . . get it.... I'm going to have to try for it!"

Bolan peered around the side of the crate, and shots rang out from three places in the cargo hold. Great, the Executioner thought. Jamison had buddies on board.

The plane tentatively left the ground, only to bounce back again, shaking the crate and moving it a foot backward toward the open hold. Bolan could hear the engines straining against the drag of the ramp.

"...end of the runway!" the pilot was screaming, and he tried to raise the plane again, this time just barely staying up.

A wrench lay on the floor near Bolan's feet. He picked it up and tossed it, timing himself for the hit. He jumped just as the thing rattled to the ground. The two gunmen and Jamison reacted immediately. They came up to shoot at the noise, and Bolan leveled his weapon, squeezing as soon as the quarry was in his sights. The man took it in the side of the head and went down bloody. The other two ducked down, and Bolan had just evened the odds by a third.

The engines whined, and Bolan saw treetops through the open hold. A branch had got caught in the ramp and broke off inside the plane.

They rose sharply then, the angle of ascent increasing to almost fifty percent as the ship bucked. And all at once unsecured freight began shifting quickly toward the back of the plane.

Bolan jumped aside as the bomb crate slid backward, jamming himself against the curved ribs of the aircraft as boxes and equipment moved quickly in his direction.

Everything was shifting, dangerously on the move. The bomb crate slid all the way back, wedging to a stop against the jeep Bolan had driven into the plane. Other boxes moved out the back of the plane and into the night.

"I can't gain altitude!" the pilot screamed into the radio. "There's too much drag!"

The second gunman was knocked down by a sliding crate. His eyes widened as he bumped against the side of the jeep and tumbled down the ramp and out. The man's screams were lost in the pitiful cry of the plane's overworked engines.

Now there was only Jamison and the pilot—and a hydrogen bomb that could go off at any moment.

The inside of the bay was lit in a red glow by the emergency lights. Bolan, holding onto the ribbing, tried to bring himself to a kneeling position to get a look, but Jamison fired whenever the Executioner showed himself.

The engines were opened to full throttle. It was the only way the pilot could keep the few hundred feet of altitude they had. And Bolan began to understand something the pilot probably already knew: they could never land this way.

Then he realized that Jamison knew it, too, and that if any of them were going to stay alive, they'd have to bail out. He rose again, holstering Big Thunder so that he could pull himself along the ribs of the aircraft with both hands.

He saw Jamison's shadow working his way along the secured freight to the cockpit door. He opened the door and disappeared.

Bolan slowly made his way toward the front of the plane. He had to somehow make sure the plane was over the sea and away from civilization before it crashed. He reached the front just as shots rang from the cockpit. Using secure rods along the front, Bolan slowly pulled himself to the door. The Pacific Ocean twinkled under a full moon below him, through the open ramp.

He made the door but couldn't draw a weapon and open the thing at the same time. Bolan grabbed the knob with both hands, and the door swung open, almost dislodging him. He grabbed the inside door frame and pulled himself up in time to see Jamison pulling a life vest and parachute off the dead pilot's body. The aircraft was now on autopilot.

He saw Bolan and growled like an animal, his own weapon a handhold away. Jamison took the chance, letting go of the seat back to grab for his gun. He lost his footing immediately and fell back to hit Bolan in the doorway.

They both tumbled through the doorway and down the inside of the cargo bay toward the open ramp. As they rolled, the man planted his teeth in Bolan's arm.

The Executioner beat him on the head with both fists as they fought for what Bolan expected was the last seconds of their lives. He dislodged the man's teeth, then broke them with a hard upper right. Bolan and Jamison rolled over and over toward the rapidly approaching open bay.

They came to the end of the hold, banging once against the bomb crate, then bouncing onto the disabled ramp itself. Bolan released the man and grabbed for a handhold. His fingertips locked in the joining crease of the ramp. He clung to the half-open door.

Jamison held on to Mack Bolan's belt. His body floated like a flag in the rushing winds. He scrabbled for a foothold, getting one knee back on the lip of the ramp. Both men pulled with all their strength toward the inside of the plane.

Bolan got a handhold on the bumper of the twisted jeep, pulling himself back up as Jamison grabbed the inner rim of the hatchway.

No sooner had they gotten inside than Jamison launched himself at Bolan again. The man's mind was gone, he was lost in a frenzy.

He attacked like an animal as both men tried to grab on to the jeep. They flailed at one another with their free hands. Bolan finally managed to get a leg planted between the busted bumper and the jeep itself.

Both hands free, he grabbed Jamison with one and pounded his head with the other. Then he lifted him bodily, like a wrestler, brought him over his head and threw the kicking animal out the back of the plane. Moonlight glinted off Jamison's uniform buttons as he fell to his death.

The Executioner turned immediately and began making his way back to the front of the plane. When he reached the cockpit, he put on the pilot's Mae West and parachute.

Bolan pulled the pilot's body out of the seat and studied the instrument panel, locating the fuel gauge, direction finder and altimeter. He knew very little about flying the plane, but native intelligence could take him as far as he needed to go.

The fuel was burning at an incredible rate, already a fourth gone. At that pace the plane wouldn't fly for long. They were sitting at just under four hundred feet, not great for jumping, but he knew he had little choice. It was heading due east, which meant there was nothing between the plane and the empty ocean except Midway Island, nearly twenty-five hundred miles away. The plane couldn't make it nearly that far the way it was burning fuel.

Bolan took a deep breath and made his way out of the cockpit, working quickly down the ribs to the open bay. He didn't want to think about it. He simply reached the ramp, opened his arms and let himself be swept away.

He became the night, floating with outstretched arms. He pulled the cord as soon as he was clear of the plane. The chute opened, jerking him violently. Bolan had about a minute to appreciate the vast emptiness of the Pacific Ocean before he, too, became a part of it.

He hit water, bobbing under. His first priority was to get out of the chute before it filled with water and dragged him under. Bolan got it unclipped and it floated away, leaving him alone.

The Executioner was down. He looked to the east. If his calculations were correct, he should soon see a brightness on the horizon. And within minutes the light of an artificial sun rose like daybreak in the east.

MACK BOLAN FLOATED ALL NIGHT, exhausted and waiting for death, wondering if he would join Junko in the place of her ancestors. He contemplated death and knew that this was the place for it as he became cold, then numb, from the water around him. If the sharks didn't get him, hypothermia would. He thought about help arriving at first, then realized that no one knew that he was down, and if they did, they'd have no idea where. And as dark, feverish visions of Junko floated in his head, he thought that death was perhaps the best thing for him now, and he prepared to give himself to it.

Bolan imagined he felt a shark bumping up against him during the night, then again later. At first he thought he was simply delirious, but the third time it came, he saw that it was a dolphin—the friend of the fisherman.

It came back several times, each time getting closer, staying longer. The sun rose, warming Bolan. The dolphin came again, and this time Bolan saw the fishing boats in the distance. He realized, in his world of opposites, that he was being saved by another sentient being, a creature that wanted nothing more than to survive. Bolan summoned his remaining strength and called for help.

Life was a beautiful thing. Mack Bolan would go on living it—and fighting for it. Somebody had to.

Mack Bolan's

PHOENIX FORCE

by Gar Wilson

The battle-hardened, five-man commando unit known as
Phoenix Force continues its onslaught against the hard
realities of global terrorism in an endless crusade for
freedom, justice and the rights of the individual. Schooled
in guerrilla warfare, equipped with the latest in lethal
weapons, Phoenix Force's adventures have made them a
legend in their own time. Phoenix Force is the free world's
foreign legion!

**"Gar Wilson is excellent! Raw action attacks
the reader on every page."**

—Don Pendleton

Phoenix Force titles are available
wherever paperbacks are sold.

PF-1

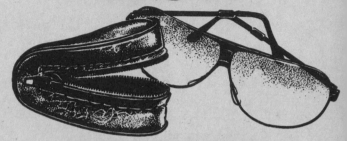